SCALP BOUNTY
Ravaging Myths, Book 2
By
Frederick Marshall Brown

Copyright 2009 Frederick Marshall Brown
Published by P450Guide.com
ISBN 0-97000-844-9

Man first occupied the Americas over a hundred thousand years ago and has survived events that led to the extinction of many other creatures on the continents. Destined to wander, he traveled in pursuit of food from other continents around the globe and ended up in the Americas like everywhere else mostly by chance. Over the millennia the influx of people migrated from the outer reaches of the Americas to the interior, slowly populating both continents. The people who eventually crossed the ice age Beringia land bridge were only some of the more recent arrivals in prehistory. Assessing this from the present, each successive wave of people could be viewed as either immigrants or invaders on their arrival in the Americas, and we may never know what their impact was on the inhabitants already present. We do know that many complex and unique cultures developed, flourished, and then disappeared over the course of time leaving mere remnants of their prior existence.

By the time the Europeans crossed the Atlantic and landed in the Americas, millions of native people with thousands of distinct cultures already occupied the two American continents. Unfortunately, the European arrivals had an absolute disregard for the people already present. Even though they were immediately struggling, the new arrivals were determined to claim what they called the 'new' and 'uninhabited' land for their already existing imperialistic countries across the ocean. The Europeans were nothing more than invaders clearly set from the start on taking the Natives' land by any necessary means even to the extent of outright genocide.

Sadly, this is what happened in our own recorded history. But the Americas did not have to evolve in that way. Changes at innumerable points in our history could have led to a tremendously altered world.

The world of Ravaging Myths traveled a different path. The native population was not decimated by European disease. The millions of natives would have fared very differently against 16th century invaders.

CHAPTER 1

The Southwestern wind blew dust devils across the road leading to the ancient native burial grounds. Swirling and whipping small particles into a frenzy, the devils did little more than cloud the otherwise unpolluted air. In mindless desperation and near silence, the sand drifted slowly across the mutilated corpse seemingly trying to bury what had been left in disgrace at the ground's edge. Sand-specked, dried blood covered the body's hairless skull, bringing further dishonor to the memory of the once proud Apache warrior. Her scalp had been viciously stripped from its bony foundation leaving clear grooves deep into the normal architecture. Like so many other killers in the distant past, the executioner had left with a trophy, bloody human flesh that was savage proof of her death. Savagery taught and encouraged by the early invaders from Europe, men who had briefly tried and failed to eradicate the natives before accepting the way of the land or leaving altogether. Savagery not practiced by the Apache, then or now.

Millennia after crossing the Bering land bridge, the Apache ancestors were driven into the North American southwest eight hundred to one thousand years ago by cataclysmic volcanic eruptions in the far north. These same major disruptions in the Pacific Rim's Ring of Fire were serious enough to cause a mass of congruent native migration to many other areas in the Americas in that distant past just as they had done for tens of thousands of years before that. The result was a heavy scatter of people with extremely different cultures to all reaches of the northern and southern continents, and what eventually would be thousands of distinct nations or tribes across the centuries.

When the Apache finally reached the southwest, many other people had already been calling it home for thousands of years, and some of them, such as the Clovis people and the ancient Anasazi had long ago come and gone from the world. The early Apache first existed as nomadic family units, appearing considerably more disorganized than most of the

other people in this new land.   They recognized no
tribal entity, so to speak, and even within in
bands there were no consistently recognized
leaders. The small groups all functioned
independently and provided for themselves
incessantly by whatever means were necessary. They
were hard-core survivors who traveled light and
lived on anything available to them in their
environment. Like most hunter and gatherer
cultures, in good times this consisted of large
game such as the deer and buffalo readily available
in the region at the time. The nomads followed the
animals as they moved between feeding grounds,
taking what they could on foot. During the worst
of times, they were able to survive by
supplementing their diet with whatever roots,
berries, nuts and seeds they could gather as they
desperately followed the game. When their very
existence was at stake, they often found it
necessary to take from their stationary and
agrarian neighbors from other tribes. Stealth and
peaceful, bloodless retreats were valued over
bloodshed, and other's lives were not taken unless
the source chose to seriously resist. Further
raids were only undertaken when the need was again
urgent. Survival was the driving force, not
uncontrolled hostility.

A half-buried machinegun and nearby bullet-
riddled military all terrain vehicle brought the
General's attention back to the twenty-first
century. She stood over the rapidly desiccating
and mutilated Apache soldier's body and tried to
identify the remains from her memories of command,
not for the Nation's records or the dead soldier's
family, but because she felt compelled to do so.
Nation, Council, and world politics aside, there
would be retaliation for this offense, both swift
and brutal. The Apache never ignored the
transgressions frequently endured or even tolerated
by others. In terms of the Apache code of honor,
the soldier's name was ultimately meaningless. The
Apache Nation's people viewed themselves as one in
the world, and had since the integration of the
Europeans centuries before. The Nation's people
being its most valuable resource, Nation insults

including the loss of a single Apache life were always avenged in kind.

Following the slow and multistage suppression of the European invasion, the Nation easily evolved with the times, continuing to absorb immigrants and their cultures with the same pride that maintained their own. After all, the Apache were and always had been flexible, utilizing superior ways whenever they presented themselves and still maintaining their own central culture. Over the centuries, this led to major advances in the abilities and holdings of the Apache Nation as well as multiple continued firm alliances with other tribal Nations of the Americas. In due course, other nations of the world also blended in to this massive and growing alliance.

The exponential growth of the Nation started with the suppression of the Spanish in the southwest and the resultant acquisition of their superior weapons and more importantly, their horses. With this greatly enhance mobility the Apache followed the ancient native trade routes that spanned the Americas, absorbing others over time that took to the Apache's nomadic ways. With hit and run guerilla tactics, the Apache gradually aided other tribes in the multi-front battle to keep their lands as they swept to the east and then north. The numbers of the Apache tribe grew with every conquest as they took prisoners instead of lives whenever they could and accepted anyone interested in a mobile and military way of life. Camps of soldiers left strategically behind in their massive sweeps grew over time and eventually became bases.

The Apache Nation now provided unparalleled protection services for its own people and its allies, a commodity invaluable in the world. In this, the Nation was never flexible. Attacks from the outside were always met in kind and without the slightest regard for diplomacy. The world knew the Apache Nation's stance regarding it people and ignorance was never accepted as an excuse. Had the Apache been ruthlessly imperialistic like the early Europeans they suppressed, they would have controlled the world long ago.

Knowing this, the General began to formulate a mental list of those bold, stupid or crazy enough to mess with the Nation. Of these three categories, the bold and the stupid had generally learned their lessons painfully in the past, with the exception of a few (clearly fitting into the combined bold and stupid subcategory).
Unfortunately, there was no shortage in the supply of crazies in the world. Crazies usually stirred up the bold and the stupid, and when these efforts failed, did a fair job of behaving bold and stupid themselves.

Overall, the murder, mutilation, and scalping of an Apache warrior, as well as the desecration of sacred grounds, Apache or not, had to be the work of a crazy. No sane person would take or pay bounty for the scalp of an Apache warrior knowing the guaranteed consequences. The acts were a deliberate attempt to rile the Nation. An Apache scalp hadn't been taken in hundreds of years. In fact, the Intertribal Council had deemed the act of scalping punishable by death well over a hundred years before now, and the edict had not changed. The Council would fully sanction the justified Apache retaliation, which would proceed whether sanctioned or not. The General found the implications of this near automatic realization disturbing at best. A single incident would purposefully bring down the wrath of the Apache Nation, the entire Intertribal Council, and every one of its allies throughout the rest of the world. The Council had already been notified, and she, the Apache tribe's Council representative, stood there now to prepare an eyewitness report of the atrocity. All that remained was the identification of those responsible and the bloody aftermath of that identification.

The Nation's surveillance satellites would have captured the killer's acts, probably unbeknownst to the perpetrator. The window of opportunity in the death had already been narrowed down to two hours by the facts that the soldier last reported in approximately twelve hours before then, and failed to report two hours later. A second failure to communicate her status brought

the soldier to command attention, and the third
failure immediately and appropriately brought it to
the General's. A unit of soldiers had routinely
been dispatched to investigate, Apache command not
anticipating a serious loss during peacetime and
also in their own heavily militarized Nation. The
unit's disturbing report brought the General there
personally, signifying a major and politically far-
reaching event. The Nation's satellite data would
be available to her in a few minutes on her
chopper. Had she not seen the end results in
person, she could have pretty much guaranteed that
she wouldn't have believed the satellite data.

Rage, and amazingly, uncertainty struggled for
control of her thoughts as she tried to assess the
situation before she had what would undoubtedly be
key pieces of data. What was this all about? Who
did this, and why? It made absolutely no sense in
the context of the current world. The Apache
Nation was incredibly strong now, possibly even
invincible. Knowingly provoking the Apache Nation
was the effective and realistic equivalent of
picking up and shaking an occupied hornet's nest,
extremely predictable and viciously dangerous. The
combined tribal strength of the Intertribal Council
and its countless global allies magnified this
beyond her comprehension. No person, group, or
nation had acted against their united strength in
twenty years, and then they had severely regretted
it. Considering all of these factors, she reached
the same conclusion over and over again. The
perpetrators and their incomprehensible acts were
insane. An endless list of good and sane people
would probably die as a result, and vengeance would
do nothing to deter the same senseless behavior in
the future until the central figures orchestrating
the murder, scalping, and desecration were
completely annihilated without the merest fraction
of a doubt.

The captain abruptly spoke, pulling her from
thoughts she could never have expected to have.
"General, the satellite data is ready for your
review, Sir."

Turning and quickly attempting to refocus her
thoughts on the here and now, she surveyed the

scene one last time. Numerous Apache men and women
of a variety of ranks and specialties were
scattered about the area and carefully processing
every detail of the site. Not even the tiniest
detail would be left undiscovered. She knew this
as certainly as she knew her own name. The
General's unquestioned confidence in the people who
diligently served under her aside, she knew without
a shadow of a doubt that they all had two things on
their minds, duty and vengeance, and not
particularly in that order.

A thin cloud drifted over the almost permanent
southwestern sun, and the shadow brought an icy
chill down her back. The grimace on the remainder
of the soldier's face told the General her story in
as much detail as she would ever get from the data
downlink from the satellite. She died gruesomely,
and had still been struggling for life when the
killer excised her scalp. Pure and unadulterated
evil emanated from the horrendous act, a sickening
new dimension added to her quick preliminary
analysis. The perp would pay immensely for every
second of the soldier's misery. And if the soldier
did not have the advantage of warrior kin, she
would personally and gladly see to the killer's
destruction herself.

She covered the short distance to the chopper
quickly with her captain dogging her heels. Even
though they were all Apache, and equals in their
Nation in that respect, the utility of the current
command structure that had been derived from that
of the European militaries was clear. Order was
absolutely necessary in any large operation, and
the Apache Nation's military was now an immensely
large interplanetary operation.

Even as a Cochise descendant, the General did
not inherit her rank; her name had been
professionally meaningless in her military career.
She earned her rank by obtaining each and every one
of her military objectives with an absolute minimum
loss of life. As with her famed Apache ancestors,
the enemy had not been so lucky. That being said,
her units worked with surgical precision, killing
and destroying only when it was necessary. As
dictated by her heritage, the General did not value

8

death or destruction. She would repeatedly back
down from a fight if necessary to spare her
soldiers' lives. There had never been honor for
the Apache in death, only in their ability to
survive. As noted before, in the Apache struggle
to survive they adapted when necessary, and
utilized everything of value without the crippling
effect of hesitation. Pride was far from relevant
in this respect. Survival was not.

Settling into her seat, she ordered, "Show me
the data, captain. Let's get this show on the
road."

"Yes, Sir." Was his instant reply.

Quickly adjusting herself to sit directly in
front of the terminal, she collected her thoughts
and prepared to view the video from the satellite
downlink. The link terminal occupied the whole
backside of the pilot's seat, and could receive any
form of data or communications necessary in the
field, whether it was full motion satellite video
such as what they expected to see then, or simple
text messages. The Apache Nation satellites were
capable of capturing digital wide range high
definition video data that could be zoomed clearly
down to a basic microscopic resolution when
conditions were good. As a result, she had visual
access to all of the happenings of the world since
the time the satellite system had been placed into
orbit. The only inputs necessary were the GPS
coordinates and the specific time frame. The
technology had greatly enhanced Apache intelligence
gathering, but had several remaining flaws that
significantly reduced the almost limitless amount
of potential data they could retrieve. First,
video could only be captured in the visual range
also viewable by the human eye. This eliminated
several useful spectra often used in short-range
intelligence gathering, such as infrared.
Fortunately, digital enhancement rendered video
data usable even in the near absence of light.
Second, and far more detrimental, was the inability
to penetrate low-level atmospheric disturbances,
otherwise known as clouds. The same could be said
for any object placed even briefly between the
satellite and the target area. Data could be

extrapolated to fill in some of the missing data, but this was by no means precise. Finally, the Nation currently lacked the processing power necessary to track movement coordinate to coordinate over time even though the data to do so was stored and available. The General had been told this would not be practical until they had completed the superconductor based processor facility on Luna's northern pole. The constant subzero temperature there would reportedly make the whole thing possible, and the data itself was already being stored near the same site on the moon. Considering all of this, the General still expected to gain some useful information from the data downlink since the site in question was in the middle of the wide-open and clear skied desert.

Suddenly, the screen lit up. The view started from the satellite's orbit elevation, and rapidly zoomed towards the earth. An interesting sight the first time anyone watched data like that, but pointless beyond that and sometimes even nauseating.

"Captain, I only want the surface view at these coordinates," The General stated in barely veiled disgust.

"Yes, Sir. I'll cut the theatrics, Sir"

"The video tech must be a damn búh." The General said with a smirk.

"Yes, Sir." The Captain responded, barely concealing a smile.

Although English had mostly supplanted the Apache language by then, the General was occasionally compelled to throw a few Apache words into her speech to test and predominantly entertain her troops. Búh was the Apache word for owl, and the captain had passed her test.

Within seconds, the view shifted to an overhead low altitude view of the local surroundings time stamped with the beginning of the window of opportunity. The area appeared desolate. The soldier hadn't even been at the coordinates initially. She had to appear on the scene eventually so the General told the captain to forward scan the data. Since nothing mobile appeared for a short time, the scene seemed unchanged.

"Captain, are you running the data forward?"
She asked.

"Yes, Sir. No activity, Sir."

"Damn waste of time."

"Yes, Sir." The captain responded, not feeling
good about the General's irritation.

Easily bored, the General's thoughts flicked
back to the past and her tribe's history. Although
the Nations were much more stable now, the early
Apache ancestors throughout the southwest brought
down the wrath of numerous other tribes in the
region due to their raiding behavior, and some of
these tribes were as fierce as her ancestors.
Apache raids justifiably provoked animosity and
retaliation from the victims who had clearly worked
hard to acquire the goods that were stolen. After
all, labors lost were not easily forgotten, and the
raid victims' own survival was also at stake. Even
during that era, however, the Apache would
occasionally form alliances with various other
nations. As would be expected, these relationships
fluctuated with time, resources, and, of course,
the behavior of the Apache. The most frequent of
these alliances were with the Pueblo, whose
villages the Apache often camped around.

The Pueblo were proud ancestors of the
Anasazi, an ancient and extremely advanced culture
that thrived in the southwest in the distant past.
The Pueblo were actually numerous distinct tribes
that had been designated 'Pueblo' by the early
Spanish invaders due to their characteristic type
of housing. But on their arrival in the early
1500's, the Spanish conquistadors did much more
than give the Pueblo a new name. They caused
dramatic changes in the ways of life of all the
southwestern tribes. Only a few of these changes,
(i.e. sheep, cattle, horses, and guns), were
ultimately of any benefit to the natives, and the
Apache took to them quickly without falling under
the spell of the Spanish.

The General returned to the mental report
being generated in her head. First, they had an
isolated location in the center of Nation
territory. Second, soldiers routinely did solo

patrol in the area for reason number one, as
evidenced by the dead soldier fifty yards away.
Third, the soldier, identity confirmed by the duty
roster as Sergeant Ilya O'Connor, had a perfectly
clean and exemplary service record. Fourth, the
soldier had been seventh generation Apache, her
family having originally emigrated from Ireland in
the 1860's. Apache lineage was matrilineal, and
the ancestry of all Nation members had been tracked
since they entered the Nation for various reasons.
A thorough scan of the Apache Nation databases
yielded no known cause for retaliation against the
soldier or her extended family. The Nation's
military maintained this retaliatory offense data
for the protective benefit of its members. The
Apache were probably the only nation on the entire
planet who kept this type of records.

"General, the sergeant has entered the field
of view."

The General's attention fell back to the
screen, which had been hypnotically unchanging only
moments before. The sergeant's Jaagé, the Nation's
fast, light duty combat unit, sat at the scene.
Jaagé was the Apache word for antelope, a suitable
comparison to the vehicle. Again the screen
stagnated, this time only different because of the
Jaagé. The effect seemed worse due to the shift
back to real time video speed, but details could
not be missed and would be electronically tagged
for fast future review.

After what felt like an hour, but could only
have been ten minutes, a soldier exited the
vehicle. Pausing and zooming the video down
specifically to the soldier confirmed the soldier's
rank and name by way of the shoulder data patch.
The patches had been implemented after the
satellite system, when it became clear every
soldier looked the same from altitude.
Unfortunately, the general public wore no such
patches, but then, they supposedly also had no
awareness of the surveillance abilities of the
Nation's satellites.

The soldier, or at least the soldier's patch,
identified, the captain pulled the view back up and
restarted the video sequence. The sergeant looked

around briefly, and then slowly walked into the burial grounds. Again, she briefly looked around, but stood stationary for several minutes afterwards. The behavior suggested she was listening intently for whatever reason, but only she would ever know this, and she would never tell. She then gradually lowered herself to her knees, and began to sift through the burial ground sand with her hands. These actions were clearly not those of an Apache, particularly one of long lineage! The Apache did not make contact with the dead, even when long turned to dust. Ghost sickness, even though a belief of the past still held tremendous sway over their thoughts and actions.

Historically, the Apache avidly avoided the dead. Following the death of a family member, only the closest male relative prepared the body, and then it was buried as quickly as possible. All personal possessions of the deceased, and even the clothing worn by the relative during the burial were then immediately burned. The dead person's wickiup, or other dwelling from early times, also came down in fire. In the earliest times, the person's name was not spoken and more importantly, the grave was avoided at all costs. Violating these beliefs could lead to haunting or even harm by the dead's ghost, i.e. ghost sickness. In modern times, the medical community had attributed ghost sickness to anxiety and depression related to grief. Both of these psychiatric illnesses were more common in close relatives of the deceased, much like the Apache ghost sickness. In addition, the destruction of the dead person's possessions and the burier's own clothes suggested elimination of a possible disease that could have led to the death. As can be seen, science had explained many things away satisfactorily, but a fear of the dead still remained. Superstition, perhaps, but deeply and probably irrevocably entrenched in the Apache culture.

The captain and the General exchanged glances. The situation there had instantly become dire by Apache standards. The behavior they had witnessed to that point indicated extreme deviance from their

normal ways, for whatever reason. The Apache were
no longer primitive, but they knew their own
people. Deliberate sifting of grave dust in a
burial ground was indicative of a very disturbed
mind, even to that day.

"Pause the video, captain!" The General said
abruptly.

As further evidence the images also disturbed
the captain, he paused the video without verbally
responding to her command. A small thing she could
easily overlook, but extremely significant all the
same.

The sergeant had no history of psychiatric
disturbance, and the records indicated none in her
lineage. In addition, there were no known witches
in her lineage. Only they, of the Apache, would
venture into this realm of behavior in the absence
of extreme mental illness, and even then, their
sanity was questionable these days. Unbelievable
as it may seem, the belief in witches still existed
in the current world, Apache and otherwise. In
spite of the advancements in science, technology,
and medicine, even the General, a seasoned military
officer, felt uncertainty in the presence of a
known witch. This uncertainty spread to other
unexplainable phenomena as well, perhaps as a
result of her cultural beliefs regarding the
spiritual world.

"What's your impression of the situation so
far, captain?" She asked.

"Sir?"

"I said what do you think happened here,
captain?"

"I can't really say, Sir." The captain said
quickly, reluctant to speak.

"Off the record, captain, what do you think?"
The General pushed on.

"Permission to speak freely, General, Sir?"
The captain now said hesitantly.

"As I said, off the record. Go ahead."

"Something's not right here, General. At
least, that's my gut feeling." The captain said,
regretting it immediately.

"What do you mean?" The General continued,
feeling she was onto something.

"I don't know how to say this exactly, but I don't think what we saw is…normal, I guess, Sir."

More encouraged by this, the General prodded him further, "Go on."

"Well, I….I didn't know the sergeant personally or anything. She's not in my unit, my clan or anything like that. But I can't see one of our people doing that... I don't know how else to say it…"

The General looked at the captain, feeling the clear uneasiness emanating from him like heat from the sun. The uneasiness being mutual, she kept stone-faced composure as expected for her rank and history. To let these 'feelings' cloud her judgment and her command would interfere with the investigation, a possibility she couldn't afford. What she observed and heard from the captain confirmed her own inner reaction, however, and that 'gut feeling' meant a great deal.

"Restart the video, captain." The General stated simply, returning her attention to the monitor.

The sergeant's movements continued for a brief time, then she abruptly stood up. With slowness suggesting she had knowledge of the satellite observation, she tilted her head back to stare at the sky directly above her. The captain sucked in a quick breath and pushed back from the monitor. The evil toothy smile glaring brightly in the sunlight was not that of the sergeant. The image abruptly went black, and stayed black for the remainder of the data window.

CHAPTER 2

The first entries of the Spanish into the North American southwest were primarily by wanderers, traders, and priests, individually mostly harmless to the native cultures there at the time. But the individuals returned to New Spain with grand stories that eventually led to invasion by the conquistadors in 1539. The second wave of invaders was far from harmless and was interested in conquest and destruction more than anything else. Of course, rumors had also led them to believe that the seven cities of Cibola were in the southwest, and the invaders were greatly interested in finding these cities of gold for obvious reasons. Under Coronado, the conquistadors met considerable resistance, but were brutal, on horseback, and had massively superior firepower. Over time, this culminated in the defeat and submission of multiple native villages, including those of the Zuni Pueblo. The cruel reputation of the Spanish led to the reluctant obedience of many other Pueblo tribes throughout the region. But eventually, Coronado and the other greedy conquistadors were tricked by the Pueblo into heading onto the Great Plains in search of their precious cities of gold. Word of the conquistadors fortunately preceded them through the extensive native trading networks, and the Pecos, Tejas, Apache, and Pawnee further tricked them along the way leading them an even greater distance out of the southwest. After a year of fruitless wandering that took them as far as the Wichita tribe on the Great Plains, Coronado returned to New Spain without a speck of gold, a very broken man.

Multiple other Spanish expeditions into the southwest from 1542 until 1590 resulted in nothing more than Catholic priests dying at the hands of wary, previously abused and now hostile natives. Time passed until 1598 when Juan de Onate, a wealthy man from New Spain, led a large number of soldiers and colonists into the southwest and claimed it as New Mexico for himself, his king, and his god. The Spanish who were intent on converting all of the supposed savages to Christianity and taking their land in the process treated the natives who continued to inhabit Onate's freshly claimed New Mexico poorly. When turned their way, this treatment quickly led to open hostility towards the Spanish from many other tribes including the Acoma, Jumano, Navajo, Tewa, Hopi, and Apache. Even with this added resistance and due predominantly to their continued superior firepower and uncontained brutality, the Spanish continued to be successful in defeating the natives, but the most stationary of the tribes, the Pueblo of course felt the greatest impact since they were trapped in the heart of Juan de Onate's unrightful claim.

In the years following the defeat of the natives, the Pueblo fell even deeper into the very controlling influence of the invading Spanish. The cruel reality was that the Pueblo tribes had absolutely no other choice because they were being forced into slavery at the hands of both the Spanish military and the Spanish priests. To further the insult, the Spanish government conveniently granted native lands to its soldiers, and the grants dictated that all inhabitants of that land immediately had to serve the Spanish owner and could no longer hold property of their own. In addition, the soldiers now expected tribute from their native slaves on a regular basis, leading to the natives being pushed to near starvation. Unfortunately, the Catholic priests were no better to the natives than the Spanish soldiers. The priests also expected slave labor in their fields and churches, but worsened the situation by demanding that the natives abandon their own spiritual beliefs and become Christians. Failure to comply with the demands of either the soldiers or the priests resulted in beatings and or death.

The Pima Indians, who had been recruited and Christianized very early in the Spanish invasion of the southwest, initially continued to help the Spanish in their colonization efforts, including in Spanish battles with the Pueblo, Navajo, and Apache. Eventually, due to the characteristic poor treatment dealt out by the Spanish in spite of their supposed Christian alliance, even the Pima returned mostly to their native ways and joined the intertribal union against the Spanish.

The loss of the last of their native allies dealt a considerable blow to the Spanish invaders. Desperately, they began to offer bounties for native scalps. The apparent idea was to stir up entrepreneurship and thereby eventually eliminate their enemies by the power of pure greed, something the Spanish knew well. This brought many unscrupulous characters into the southwest hoping to gain scalp bounty Spanish gold at the expense of native lives. But the bounties were repeatedly and uselessly increased due to the difficulty of the task. In spite of the large bounties paid, few would brave the combined ferocity of the southwestern tribes. Ultimately, the Spanish were driven out of the region and never again obtained a stronghold in the southwest.

The early morning Phoenix sun poured heat onto the southwestern desert sand as John Clandridge climbed into his small 2-seater plane. His unusually careful preflight checks done, he would be in the air in a couple of minutes winging towards Pueblo Bonito for the hundredth time since he had taken up flying. He had been on the Intertribal Council serving the Pima Nation now for 37 years, longer than most of his fellow Council members by decades. Over that time, he had seen Council members come and go like dust in the wind, always keeping careful note of the resultant mood shifts in the Council as a whole. He had gotten to be a pretty good politician during those years, and his people seemed to respect his abilities. Having been born into a family of Pima farmers 72 years ago, he had fallen into politics at the local level early on in his life in response to Apache threats to his family business. The world just didn't seem to be big enough for the Apache, and they had swallowed countless other nations in their apparent drive for dominance. From his perspective, these efforts had gone global at this point, and it had become difficult to keep track of the holdings of the Apache Nation. His interventions on the Council years before had prevented the Pima Nation from being lost in the shuffle, but he was always on guard for further shifts in the Pima direction, and had difficulty refraining from open hostility with the many Apache council representatives that he had outlasted through the years. Council member Cochise had been no exception to this up to this point in her tenure, and it was unlikely that her style would change. Ancient Pima-Apache differences aside, she simply glowed with the nasty characteristics he had long attributed to members of the Apache Nation as if she were a poster child for their ways. Bold, ruthless, and unforgiving, he had learned to abhor the Apache over his years on the Council much like his Pima ancestors had in the past, and the sudden urgency of this Council meeting she had called didn't bring her closer to his heart by any means. With the flight ahead of him, he gradually withdrew his thoughts from the anger he felt towards the Apache, and settled back into the routine that had carried him safely to Pueblo Bonito so many times in the past. Several hours of relaxing flight time later, he noted the small jet heading for a landing ahead of him at Pueblo Bonito, and recognized it as Apache Nation Military. His stress level instantly skyrocketed, and he decided to stay in the air for a little longer to avoid Cochise at the airport. He would be in her presence more than enough in the near future.

As the small Apache jet circled to land, the General calmly observed the view from above the ancient Pueblo Bonito ruins and was amazed as always by the remains. The abilities of the Anasazi a thousand years ago competed easily with other cultures of that time around the world. The giant D-shaped construction, which contained over 650 rooms and stood five stories tall, was not duplicated in size in America until the nineteenth century. The remains of the structure were still impressive even though time had taken its toll.

The decision to locate the Western Intertribal Council Building near the Anasazi site had been commendable from the General's perspective. Being one of North America's oldest and most advanced native population centers with still existing large-scale ruins, it served as a great reminder of the ancestors. She felt it was always an honor to return there.

Triggered by the ruins to return to her reflections on the past, the General was soon swallowed in her train of thought from the day before in regard to the unfortunate Pueblo. While the Pueblo were being enslaved in the midst of the

Apache and Navajo back then, both of the more mobile tribes gradually acquired resources by various means from the Spanish and their captives. As a result of the injustices constantly dealt out by the Spanish, many Pueblo fled into the realms of the Navajo and varied Apache tribes. Since they often fled with horses and livestock, the Pueblo were always welcomed, and in this way, they contributed to the acquisition of animals by the free tribes. Both the Apache and the Navajo tribes quickly became adept at managing these new resources, and further increased their stock by raiding the Spanish and their Christianized Pueblo who were not interested in escaping Spanish control.

As more and more Pueblo escaped from the Spanish cruelty, the Spanish responded by raiding the Apache and Navajo to reacquire their horses, livestock, and Pueblo slaves. Of course, captured Navajo and Apache were also pushed towards slavery and Christianization, but they had no desire for either. All out war soon commenced, and over several decades, hostilities escalated multiple times in efforts to drive the Spanish invaders out of the southwest. During this period, the Spanish frequently betrayed their native allies by raiding them to obtain new slaves, and by doing so they provoked more tribes into the alliance against them.

Eventually, after about eighty years, the brutal, slave-trading ways of the Spanish finally became intolerable to even the most loyal Christianized Pueblo. As the Spanish attempted to continue their control, these Pueblo at last found they had an enemy worth a true alliance with the Apache and the Navajo. Under the leadership of the Pueblo medicine man, Popé, the tribes drove the Spanish out of the Pueblo strongholds in 1680. Following the revolt, the Spanish, unwilling to give up, continued to provide a mutual enemy, as well as a source of provisions for the allied tribes. As such, the Spanish presence also continued to bring peaceful coexistence to the Navajo and numerous Pueblo and Apache tribes.

Still within view of the ruins, the General's thoughts returned again to the present as the superstructure of the modern Council building sitting next to and dwarfing Pueblo Bonito caught her attention. The massive building complemented the other two Intertribal Council Buildings located at Cahokia and Chichen Itza, all if combined forming a complete circle. As should be obvious, prominent early Native American cultural sites in what was now North America were chosen as building sites. Cahokia had been the home of the Mississippians, temple mound builders whose work remained next to the Council Building-East. Chichen Itza once stood as a major population center of the Maya, hence was the site of Council Building-South. The selection of the southern site was apparently more difficult and required considerable thought by the Council. Both the Aztec and the Inca also had prominent cultural centers in North and South America. Aside from the small point that the Spanish had totally conquered and decimated both of them, the selection process of the southern site still remained a mystery to her even now that she was on the Council. Although the Council Building completions occurred only eight years before, the General did not have the honor of serving on the Council at the time.

The General's arrival on the landing strip usually brought a single vehicle to the side of the jet just off the runway. Familiar with procedure, she exited the jet and waited for the shuttle to arrive. By shuttle, she really meant a Só-qui-li, the Cherokee word for horse. This being a large, utilitarian transport vehicle, it suited its name, just like the Jaagé. The people of the Nations were apparently simple minded when it came to naming their vehicles.

The Cherokee Nation was responsible for a large portion of the vehicles produced in the Nations, both military and otherwise. The Cherokee were also responsible for most of the advances in science and technology that had occurred both there and in the world as a whole. The General felt, without envy, that this was due to their extensive worldwide business affiliations more than to intellectual superiority. Being nearer the east coast, they experienced a larger influx of immigrants early on, and these immigrants brought knowledge and advancements not available to the Apache until much later. But had the Apache and other early members of the Intertribal Council not intervened on their behalf, the Europeans would have suppressed and abused them much the way the Spanish worked against The Apache in the southwest. At the time, they were apparently oblivious to the potential threat, having worked out supposed trade deals that gave them a false sense of security.

It was clear the Apache Nation held its own in ways other than that of the Cherokee. But even then, the Apache quickly expanded on the uses of many technologies they had developed in collaboration with the Cherokee. Though greatly different, the Cherokee were now kin to the Apache. The General was proud to say so, and would defend them with her life.

Within minutes, the Só-qui-li pulled up next to the General. Her driver, a lieutenant in the Apache Nation, was stationed there at Pueblo Bonito along with most of his extended family. The Apache made great efforts to keep family units, even bands and clans, together when doing assignments. As such, assignments were generally long-term and carefully selected for at all times to insure mutually beneficial results for everyone involved. They were fortunate in that regard because lineage frequently carried genetic aptitudes and interests held by many in the same family unit or band.

The Apache Nation, being the predominant military Nation in the Intertribal Council, attracted like-minded individuals to its number like the other Nations did in their own respects. The members of the Apache Nation who excelled at different, non-military aspects of life usually left the Nation and became members of the Nation most suited to them. This happened most frequently by marriage, but could occur at any time without restriction or any adverse consequences. In this way, the Nations were very fluid, and blood kinship was indeed present between all the Nations and in fact, throughout most of the world.

The Navajo, of Athapascan descent like the many divisions of the Apache, in time had formed a fairly tight bond with them. By doing so, they capitalized on the skills of both tribes, which were actually similar in so many ways. During this cultural co-integration, the Apache adopted the clan system of the Navajo, it being only a small extension of the band system they already utilized. With the multitude of prior alliances formed by each tribe, the clan structure meant the Apache now had extended family connections stretching across the continent. Since the Apache never attacked or stole from their own, the intertribal alliance successfully put an end to their raids against the other native tribes. Before the eventual European integration, the white invaders were not so fortunate.

Although the Apache and the Navajo shared similar Athapascan descents, they remained single tribes each forming a separate Nation. Many individual tribes formed their own Nations in similar ways. Within some Nations, however, culturally similar tribes combined, and yet the tribes remained distinct, just very like-minded. The Pueblo Nation, with its many small tribes, was one such example. They remained Apache allies following the defeat of the Spanish, and even though they shared similar territory to the Navajo and Apache, they became three separate nations. But even in the combined tribe Nations, each tribe had a representative in the Intertribal Council, and every tribe had an equal vote regardless of its size. Representatives were selected by various means from within the tribes, and the representatives presented to the Council Building nearest their Nation.

Technology allowed the representatives in the three distant Council Buildings to all appear together and interact real-time via a holographic projection of each distant site's Council Chamber onto the local Building where the real representatives met. The Intertribal Council Buildings were built as three complimentary portions of a giant circle with this technology in mind. It was very effective and almost unnerving

in its realism. The General's own first experience
with it almost gave her a heart attack as the other
Council members suddenly appeared as if by magic
before her. She chose to believe other newly
elected representatives had been equally affected.

"Lieutenant, take me to the office. I need
time to prepare for the Council meeting."

"Yes, Sir, General Cochise."

As was indicated before, the General did not
make rank due to her name. The name was mostly
withheld to this point because it tended to serve
as a distraction. The General's maternal great,
great, great grandfather was the Cochise known to
the Nations' history. He was a great warrior and
general who served proudly in the Nation's military
during and after the massive slave trader revolts
of the 1830s. The slave trader wars were very
disruptive to the Intertribal alliance in spite of
the fact that many of its own Native people had
been captured and treated as slaves before the
European integration. Cochise and many others
fought valiantly at the time to bring freedom to
all, whether they were Native, European, or African
in descent. The southern slavers' resistance was
intense, but the antislavery factions of the
Council ultimately won out and permanently
eliminated slavery in all sectors of the
Intertribal domain.

Understanding the severity of that past
situation, the General believed that her ancestor
would have succeeded in the present time as he had
in his own. Even without considering him, the
Apache Nation still abounded with similar very
capable individuals, and she was only one of them.
She believed mere remnants of Cochise's abilities
had been passed down to her through her lineage.

The General's full name was Andrea Dicus
Cochise. She was not the first female Apache
general, and would not be the last. In the tribe's
early history, Apache women did not involve
themselves with actual combat and retaliation, but
did play a major role in the danger of raids by
acting as decoys during the acquisition of raid
bounty. Women also held prominent roles in the
decision making process within bands and as already

noted previously lineage was matrifocal. Contact
with other tribes over the course of time,
particularly the Iroquoian tribes of the northeast
and southeast, such as the Cherokee, brought women
even further to the forefront. As time progressed
and the Nation became heavily oriented towards the
military, women naturally became equal members of
the military organization. In fact, the Apache had
a long history of female/male equality not seen in
other cultures around the world until much later.

In terms of the General's name, the Apache
adapted to the European style of naming, with
slight modification, due to its usefulness in
documenting and preserving lineage. Her last name
was from her mother's lineage. Her middle name was
the last name of her father's maternal line rather
than some meaningless extra name. Again, the
Apache were adaptable, and it might be added, very
practical.

The Dicus line of the General's heritage
arrived on the east coast of America early in the
Euro-invasion. Apparently, they quickly became
known as Black Dutch, a derogatory term that made
note of their intermarriage with local natives.
The General couldn't be sure of the tribe that
became part of her Dicus heritage, but would have
guessed it to be either Algonquin or Iroquoian due
to the region. She still liked to believe it
factored into the person she had become.

The drive to the Council Building went quickly
as she mentally gathered the various portions of
her investigation into a coherent story. The
information gathered in the past two days answered
many of the early questions she had developed at
the burial grounds. Data was still accumulating
now as the initial findings were further evaluated.
In fact, Captain Atwell was camping at the site
with a team to protect its integrity until they
determined no further data needed to be acquired
there. The General was sure of the captain's
abilities, but it also had to be noted that the
team was armed to the teeth. The Nation was not
sure yet why that particular site was chosen for
the body dump, but could pretty much guarantee that
his efforts would prevent it from happening there

again.

In spite of the Apache Nation's attempts to keep the incident relatively quiet, the call for an immediate Council meeting triggered alarm so great that preliminary findings had to be divulged. Unlike the Council members' subordinates, the Council members themselves did not reside permanently near the Council Buildings. Council member duties required them to stay in touch with their varied tribal interests. In addition, most of them had maintained their roles held in society before they were named Council members. In the General's case, she maintained reduced, but active status in the Apache Nation's military, and would lead her troops into war if necessary at any time. Even so, the overall result of an emergency meeting was sometimes abrupt abandonment of ongoing projects, a hardship that was very seldom placed on the Council members.

The preliminary data the Apache Nation reported to the Council representatives brought understanding and quick responses from them all. At the time, the Nation could only absolutely confirm the dead soldier's identity, cause of death, and of greatest concern to the Council, the scalping and sacred ground violations. The General wasn't sure whether they were more upset by the violations, or the idea that they occurred in the heart of the Apache Nation under the noses of their primary military and protective force. She suspected the latter and doubted she was wrong.

On arrival at the Council Building, two others members of the General's staff met her at the entrance. Both Colonel Victorio and Private Smith had gone the past thirty-six hours without sleep, and they visibly showed the effects of the pressure they were under to assist in her analysis of the situation.

"General, we've received the most recent data from Intelligence. I don't think you'll be very happy with what they've determined."

"What do you mean, Colonel? I just had an update before takeoff. How different could their results be now?"

"That's why I don't think you'll be happy,

Sir. May I speak freely, Sir?"

"Of course, Colonel. You know you can.
You've been one of my closest advisors for the past
year."

"Well, General. After a shitload of
rationalizations, they admitted they screwed up in
their first assessments."

"What?"

"They screwed up, General, I kid you not."

"How did they manage to do that? The info we
sent them from the site was pretty straight
forward."

"I taped their transmission, General. I think
you should wait to see it for yourself."

Pushing through her office door, the General
saw the Intelligence logo already cued up on her
wall-sized monitor. Without even sitting down, she
started the report.

The Intelligence logo immediately disappeared
and an analyst filled the screen. The analyst,
Colonel Oldham, had been involved with Intelligence
for a long time, and the General knew him well.
They weren't exactly on the best of terms. They
had suffered a small command dispute a few years
before when the General ordered him to provide her
with classified data to present to the Council.
Oldham refused. Being both Council and military,
the General threatened to bust his rank, and he
reluctantly provided the data. She had a feeling
that pride stood in the way a little, or at least
that and his near absolute control of Intelligence
at the time. He had been the highest-ranking
officer in Intelligence then; a career colonel
stuck at his rank due to a lack of field duty.
Oldham resented the General and resented her
ability to order him around. But that wasn't her
problem, or at least not until it got in the way of
her need to serve the Nation and the Council.
Oldham was originally of the Navajo Nation, and
unfortunately, still carried on a centuries old
family grudge against General Cochise's ancestors.
She didn't even know the details, and usually
couldn't really care less. She continued to
believe that the people in the Nation were all kin
now, and should be working together as such.

Whatever may have happened then would most likely not have happened in today's world. Some day, when she had absolutely nothing else to do, she would search the database and see if the transgression had been recorded, even though highly unlikely. Any serious offense would have been appropriately dealt with at the time, leaving the grudge a pitiful excuse for his shitty attitude towards her.

With this as an unfortunate foundation, she watched the video and prepared for the worst. Colonel Oldham came to life, and began the rationalizations Victorio warned her about.

"General, during the absence of two of my most important analysts, we evaluated the data from the satellite as requested, and have previously presented the results to you. As I noted, we were understaffed, and lacked the insight of my best people in that analysis. You are aware of those conclusions, and we felt one hundred percent confident in the validity of our assessment at the time, otherwise I would not have reported to you as I did. Since the return of the staff I mentioned, the importance of several details that were previously undervalued has come to light. I still stand by my previous analysis in the absence of information relating to the newly identified fragments of data."

Glancing to her right, the sneer on the Colonel's face told her a great deal about the importance of the 'data fragments' Oldham was trying to minimize. Since he was also well aware of the new conclusions, she settled into a chair to watch the remainder of the video. At that point, she had two hours to prepare for the Council meeting emergently scheduled only a day before. Oldham really pissed her off and there wasn't a damn thing she could do about it except sit and listen to the bastard until he was finished.

In the General's anger her thoughts again drifted briefly, this time to the origins of the Council. Over the course of many decades, a large number of other tribes in the Southwest joined the Apache-Navajo-Pueblo alliance. Most adopted raiding behavior to stave off the Spanish incursion and to sustain their needs. The regimented Spanish

were ill prepared for this progressive onslaught of
guerilla warfare. Unlike the previous conquests
the Spanish encountered on their arrival in the new
world such as the more organized and stationary
Aztecs and Inca, the Apaches and their allies would
not be conquered.

Eventually the alliance won out over the
Spanish. Unfortunately, the intertribal alliance
suffered a setback at that point. Without a common
enemy, tribal differences and old squabbles began
to resurface. The Apache, Pueblo, Navajo and most
other tribes gradually headed off again on their
own less than friendly pursuits. This process was
relatively slow, since the various nations gained
mutual respect for the ferocity of their allies'
during the attacks against the Spanish. The seeds
of intertribal peace had been sown, even if in very
poor soil.
Fortunately, all that had been previously gained in
terms of unity was not lost. During the alliance,
some of the larger nations peacefully absorbed many
smaller tribes that had been diminished somewhat by
illness and Spanish attacks. Following these
integrations, the new blood further tempered the
hostility among the larger tribes as a result of
the introduction of new alliances long held by
their smaller cohorts.

The Native Americans, far more sophisticated
than acknowledged by the Europeans, had
participated in transcontinental trade routes for
centuries. Through this network of trade, they
acquired many items not available to them in their
own immediate surroundings. To the detriment of
the invading Europeans, they also exchanged a large
amount of useful information in this way and
further developed intertribal alliances. When the
southwestern tribes heard of the Spanish presence
in the North American southeast and the entrance of
other even more aggressive Europeans to the north
and west of the Spanish, the new common enemy
eventually brought them back into a strong
alliance. In time, many eastern tribes affected
directly by the invasion also joined the alliance.
As such, the invasion and cruelty of the early
European settlers in the east further accelerated a

far-reaching intertribal peace.

When the European invaders were gradually suppressed, the clear benefit of intertribal alliances was observed by the various nations. The recruitment of the Iroquois Confederation, an alliance already formed on the basis of freedom, respect, tolerance, consensus, and brotherhood further strengthened the intertribal alliance and stretched it all the way across the continent even though there were some early problems between the Iroquois and their sworn enemies. The earliest incarnation of the Intertribal Council formed as a result and eventually formulated an honor code based on that of the well-organized Iroquois. Consequently, all, including the Apache, were honor bound to uphold the alliance even when historic rivalries resurfaced intermittently throughout the following centuries.

CHAPTER 3

The two hours after her arrival in her office flew by, and since the General was barely able to finish preparations before the meeting, her heart was now pounding with anxiety. Her world had changed in Sonora, and now the rest of the Council would also realize the implications of what she currently stood ready to tell them. Taking her assigned seat, she made an attempt to relax before the other Council sites appeared before the Western Intertribal Council. Many of her representative colleagues at the West site made small attempts to gather information from her before the meeting actually began, but she held her tongue. What she had to say needed to be heard by everyone at the same time to hopefully avoid the chaos of speculation that a partial release of data would detrimentally induce.

Precisely on time, the projections from the other two Building sites simultaneously appeared before her. She couldn't see a single empty seat at either of the other two Council sites. Like they had at her own Council chamber, the representatives at the other sites had all arrived unusually early in anticipation of her findings. With dark humor, she thought they would not be disappointed.

Following some brief formalities, all fell silent as General Cochise stood and began.

"Fellow tribal representatives, I, General Cochise of the Apache Nation, Apache tribe, have requested this emergency meeting of the Council, as you are all well aware. I value your time, as you should know by now, and would not presume to waste it on meaningless talk. As such, the information I have to present will be given succinctly, and without comment or speculation on my part until I am finished. Please do not begin to comment or speculate yourselves until I have finished. The floor will be open to your comments at that time."

A brief rumble of voices shook her Council chamber, as she was sure it did in the other two distant chambers. She waited a few minutes for it to die down, and then began.

"First, my decision to disclose the following information was questioned by some in my Nation. I, however, feel honor-bound to provide you with any absolutely confirmed data that may impact your tribes as it has impacted mine. As you have been made aware, a soldier and member of my Nation and tribe, Sergeant Ilya O'Connor, failed to report, as required, two days ago and was subsequently found murdered. The confirmed details of the sergeant's history and murder are as such:"

"The sergeant's body was identified to absolute certainty by dental records, fingerprints, and DNA analysis with the DNA compared to her known Nation held samples. The sergeant was an exemplary soldier. There were no black marks on her record."

The General paused briefly, but all three chambers were as quiet as the burial ground where the sergeant had been left mutilated. She proceeded with the report.

"The sergeant had no retaliatory offenses documented in the Apache Nation's extensive database; hence, it was unlikely she had enemies within the intertribal union predisposed to a crime of this nature. The sergeant's family record was equally clear of known retaliatory offenses."

This brought another rumble of speech to the Pueblo Bonito chamber, as well as the other two in Cahokia and Chichen Itza. The General had expected this. The Nation's documentation of retaliatory offenses wasn't exactly highly regarded by most of the other tribes, and some of them had determined it was evidence of the Apache's supposed unforgiving and ruthless nature. The Pima were avidly among these detractors, and as she glanced towards Council member Clandridge, she felt the heat of his gaze on her as he angrily spoke to his neighboring Council members. Clandridge had an attitude problem that wouldn't survive the Apache military. The Nation's preliminary assessment of the potential that its allies had harmed them was perhaps insulting, but well justified from her experience. She refocused her thoughts, and continued with her report.

"The sergeant was killed without a struggle and no defensive wounds were found on her body. The sergeant's cause of death was cardiac tamponade, which was due to massive blunt force trauma to the chest causing cardiac rupture and accumulation of blood in the pericardial sac. The instrument of death was not found at the scene, but was suspected to be a large mallet."

The chambers were again mostly silent. The General prepared for the uproar to come with her next statement.

"The sergeant's scalp was taken before she died."

As she had expected, all hell broke loose. The noise in the Western chamber was almost deafening, and mixed with the amplified outrage from the other two chambers, she felt the onset of a headache almost instantly. The divisive nature of her earlier statements crumbled and blew into the wind of their now strong intertribal alliance. The act hit at the heart of every Council member present in the three chambers, and the simplest way to describe the reaction was pure rage. The taking of a scalp was an abomination in the eyes of the Council and the individual Nations and tribes it represented. The act had been punishable by death for over a century, and it had been nearly that long since a single incident had even been documented. Maybe it was only a projection on her part, but she felt unity in the ferocity of the response. She also sensed the atmosphere had greatly changed, and it was no longer just the death of a solitary Apache soldier she was reporting on, but an insult to the world at large. For whatever reason, this made it easier for her to proceed, and following an extensive and rowdy delay, she was finally able to resume her report.

"The sergeant was killed at a site different from where she was dumped and eventually found, and the killer left no trace evidence on the sergeant's body or at the burial ground where the body was found." Taking a quick breath, she went on. "The sergeant's Jaagé served as the killer's means of transport to the burial ground, and only the sergeant's own blood was found in the Jaagé. The sergeant's body suffered no other trauma than what I have already described"

Again, a muffled silence held the three chambers as the General paused and prepared to finish her report.

"The killer either wore the sergeant's uniform during transit, or more likely, wore a different although similar uniform with counterfeit details, and as a result no trace evidence was found on the sergeant's uniform."

The General knew that her next revelations would bring a mix of both renewed disgust and distrust of the Apache Nation, and further indignation at the offensiveness of the killer. But she had to push on with her account regardless of the escalating pandemonium.

"The killer was observed via satellite arriving at the burial grounds in the sergeant's Jaagé. The killer was also observed exiting the sergeant's Jaagé and sifting through burial ground soil with his bare hands."

As an Apache, the General felt the absolute incongruity of this last action with her own culture and beliefs. She didn't believe she was prepared for the horror this caused among the hundreds of Council members present at the three

33

Council sites. As has been noted, the fear of the dead and ghost sickness is pervasive among the Apache tribe. The response of the Council members as a whole greatly reinforced her concerns, and indicated that the Apache beliefs were not unique.

Without waiting for the tumult to die down, the General quickly finished her report

"The killer's face was digitally captured via satellite when he looked up toward the sky, and the killer's facial details did not match any known individual in our database. The killer then left the scene by unknown means, leaving the Jaagé at the site. The satellite's ability to record data was effectively terminated for approximately one hour at that point and then again enabled. The satellite has been recording data appropriately since then without intervention on our part. Our only conclusion to account for the blackout at this point is that the computer system of the Apache Nation's Intelligence Services was effectively hacked to disable the satellite. We have only the barest minimum of an electronic trail, and no idea how the system was hacked."

"In summary, several major incidents have occurred by an unknown assailant. The assailant appeared to be experienced, methodical, and capable of both terrible and inconceivable things. The assailant's ability to infiltrate our systems threatens our security and that of everyone we protect and serve. I now open the floor to you, my fellow tribal representatives."

A sudden thunderous roar of voices ended the silence that had been absolute during the close of the General's presentation. The cumulative effect of the information she had presented created instant chaos among her peers. The implications of what she revealed would be impossible for the other Council members to grasp this quickly, but she felt no obligation to venture into that territory for them. They would most likely unveil implications she could not even dream of, and therefore she sat down to await a calm and organized response from the other representatives. Unfortunately, she had to wait a very, very long time.

For the remainder of the day, verbal confusion

filled the Council Chambers. The General tried to
focus on various conversations taking place around
her, but never entered into any herself. She saw
no one leave the rooms the entire time. Had the
assailant wished to eliminate all of the tribal
representatives in one swoop, he would have had a
large window of opportunity, supposing he could
manage to destroy three very separate sites all at
once. The thought brought a little anxiety. She
still had no ability to conceptualize his motives.
Perhaps that was his agenda. The idea crawled into
her stomach, and caused her to fidget in her seat.
Knowing no better way to deal with it and seeing no
end to the chaos around her, she stood up and
yelled for order.

"REPRESENTATIVES OF THE COUNCIL.
REPRESENTATIVES, PLEASE. MAY WE HAVE ORDER"

The General's efforts were pointless. The
disorder continued without even a slight dip in
volume. She observed no one making any effort to
assist her in producing order. She still felt
compelled to do something, so she left the Council
Chamber and headed for her office. The hell with
it, the deed was done, and the fallout would
eventually reach her wherever she went. No need to
wait in silence for what would inevitably be a
barrage of shocked accusations leveled towards the
Apache Nation and her specifically. The bubble had
burst, and it was full of napalm. The damage would
spread beyond containment by the end of the day,
and all that remained for her to do was watch.
Perhaps the others had been right about her
proposed full disclosure…

No, no second-guessing. She had to rely on
her own judgment, and needed to feel confident in
it now. Too many things to do, and no time to
waste dwelling on what couldn't be undone. She had
not perpetrated the acts, and should not be held
accountable for simply revealing the facts,
disturbing as they were.

The General's staff received word of her fiery
crash before she arrived back at the offices.
Nothing shocking about that, the representatives in
the Council Chamber could be heard throughout the
entire building, poor job of soundproofing to say

the least. But then, the sound came from the
equivalent of three full Council Chambers.
Considering that, maybe they hadn't even heard her
appeal for order. But that was pointless second-
guessing again. She had to get beyond this, and
the best way to do it from her perspective was to
catch and eliminate the sergeant's killer.

It took most of the day for the commotion in
the Council Chambers to die totally down, and the
Council either didn't notice the General's absence,
or didn't care that she had left the room. Not a
single representative contacted her following all
the commotion she had provoked. Not even her
fellow southwestern representative from the Navajo
Nation stopped by her offices to discuss the
meeting. She was extremely disappointed, and would
possibly never get out of bed again if she ever
made it there again. All in all, after a lengthy
night of Intelligence input, data analysis, and
strong coffee, she could honestly say she felt much
better about the current situation.

First of all, she had withheld many pieces of
data from her presentation because they weren't
absolutely confirmed, and as such, qualified as
speculation from her perspective. This large block
of 'speculation' yielded positively confirmed facts
over the course of the night. Among these results
was the site where the killer took out the
sergeant. They had expected the site to be between
the location of her last report and the burial
ground. They had been nearly correct in that
expectation, and close enough to locate the site
without too much trouble. The site was currently
being processed.

During the wait for the meeting to finally
quiet down, she also heard from Intelligence
regarding the hacked satellite. Following another
spew of excuses, Oldham reported a minor
breakthrough in the analysis of the killer's
identity. Actually, what they determined following
intensive review was that the assailant was wearing
a mask when he or she looked up at the sky. This
explained why they had no hits in the facial
analysis of the image, and also why the smile

seemed a little too big for the average human face. Unfortunately, it also increased the field of potential suspects to include the entire world instead of just those with a tremendously garish smile.

When her soldiers identified the murder site, she got the satellite recordings for the coordinates, and spent most of the night watching it and waiting for something to happen. The window of time she selected was maybe a little to long, but she couldn't afford to miss any details before or after the killing. She guessed she could have let someone else do it, but she felt an obligation to the sergeant and her family.

Overall, her sleepless night was well spent. The satellite had not been hacked during this earlier recording, for whatever reason. As a result, she had the unfortunate benefit of being in a front row seat to witness the entire sequence of the murder. In detail, she observed the killer arrive at the coordinates a full twenty minutes before the sergeant appeared in her Jaagé. The killer wore an Apache Nation military uniform complete with a sky view shoulder data patch. The patch indicated the killer was Sergeant Ilya O'Connor. Only that single person appeared at the coordinates prior to the arrival of the sergeant. She could not effectively tell where that person came from because she lost resolution as she zoomed out to widen her field of view. Due to this, she requested coordinate data for a small sweep of coordinates north of her primary data points, the general direction the killer had come from. Several attempts on her part to review this data over the appropriate time frame resulted in nothing. Analysis of this kind would take considerably more manpower until the Luna processors were functional and able to do the job for them.

The killer appeared to be fully aware of the sergeant's routine while on duty. In fact, he appeared to be directly in her driving path, and merely stood and waved to get the sergeant's attention. As would be expected, she stopped to assist one of her fellow soldiers apparently stranded in the desert. The killer took immediate advantage of the situation, beckoning the sergeant out of the Jaagé as if he needed assistance she couldn't provide him from inside the vehicle. When they were barely clear of the Jaagé, he abruptly turned and hit her full force in the chest with what could only be described as something black. The sergeant stumbled backward, clearly stunned by the blow. She then fell to her knees, grasping her chest. The killer stood over her, and watched as she continued to hold her chest. After several minutes, the sergeant began to wobble slightly from side to side. At that point, the killer grabbed her by the hair and used something in his other hand with a minimum of apparent effort. Within seconds, he removed her hair and the extent of his cuts became evident by the gleam of her skull. He then kicked her backwards and held her detached scalp over her face. The expression the General saw on the sergeant's face quickly took her back to the burial ground. The sergeant's face had not changed. O'Connor was now dead, her killer brutal and sadistic. The General wanted vengeance for this loss, slow … and also brutal.

General Cochise gained little else from the video. The killer moved out of her field of view briefly, and returned with something like a plastic tarp. He rolled her up in it, hauled her to the Jaagé, and placed her in the passenger seat. She never caught a glimpse of his face, masked or otherwise. In fact, the overhead view didn't even allow her to determine the sex of the killer. The only new data she gathered, in fact, was that there was only one person at the scene other than the sergeant. Whether accomplices waited beyond her field of view remained a mystery.

The General obtained the night's final piece of useful data actually near sunrise. It was this data that lifted her mood, and changed her perspective regarding the killing and the killer. With careful analysis, she believed it would lead her in the right general direction towards the ID of the killer.

When at the burial grounds, she described the old Apache beliefs concerning the dead. In spite of themselves, they had difficulty even today shedding those fairly irrational fears. But what the Apache lacked in rationality in this matter, they often made up for in courage. The dead had to be properly buried after all, and that didn't happen on it's own. Those most likely to fall to ghost sickness, the closest relatives of the deceased, consistently carried this burden. With this in mind she assumed, Captain Atwell overcame his innate fear of the supernatural, and went beyond the surface evaluation of the burial ground performed by his site processing team. First, he carefully viewed the surface details near the killer in the burial ground on the satellite video. He then went personally into the burial ground and began to excavate where the killer sifted with his bare hands. The captain wore gloves and used tools of course, but his efforts in overcoming the Apache's natural dread were admirable. She thought this partly because she didn't believe he was crazy, but in all honesty, mostly because he produced useful results. She still reserved her right to order a psychiatric eval.

Since she hadn't questioned the captain in regard to his rational, the General was unaware of his reasons for suspecting what he found. She observed the actions of the killer herself, and maybe had been too horrified at the time to carefully consider his behavior. Apparently, what appeared to be random sifting motions at the time were far more purposeful. It made sense really. In her viewing of two video sequences of the killer, he had not yet demonstrated a lack of efficiency in his actions. Other than his short wait for the sergeant, he wasted no time on meaningless activities. Even his method of killing her appeared to be relatively quick, and yet tortuous. The sergeant, no doubt, felt the pressure in her chest build as the blood filled the pericardial space and ultimately ended her heart's ability to fill and pump blood.

During the course of the captain's excavation, several soldiers new to the Apache tribe assisted him without even the slightest concern for their own safety. Both of these men were reportedly of more recent European descent, and had no misgivings about the burial ground or its contents. For these same reasons, the Nation mostly had more recent immigrants serving in the areas of duty associated with the dead. In fact, when she factored only for this specific aspect of available duty, she didn't believe a single Apache of long tribal lineage served in fields ranging from death scene investigation to mortuary sciences. Considering this, she decided she would definitely have the captain undergo a psych evaluation.

All of that aside, what the men found was both potentially very useful, and definitely intriguing. Meticulous excavation of the reported area revealed the presence of several very small squares of apparently identical size and shape, all composed of a hard, off-white material similar to bone. All of the pieces were found directly under the spot where the sergeant's body was abandoned. The pieces were also so small that the captain believed he would have missed them altogether, or mistook them for burial remnants had one of them not punctured and then been trapped in his glove. In total, the men have found seventeen of the squares at this point, and are continuing to carefully filter the dust in case more were left behind. They wouldn't be able to even begin speculation on the purpose of the pieces until they had been carefully analyzed. Until then, she could at least say that the pieces must have some significance to the killer. The objects were found only where he moved the soil, and the captain reported the depth was consistent with the shallow sweeps documented by the satellite video. The little squares were an interesting twist in an investigation that was otherwise mostly devoid of physical findings.

CHAPTER 4

Following a lag of several days, the fallout from the General's revelations to the Council was starting to accumulate. She assumed they had to perform analyses of their own potential danger due to the Apache breach in security. She had really expected an earlier backlash, but she guessed the other tribes and nations lacked the Apache Nation's well-practiced abilities in terms of risk assessment.

The General had returned to El Paso in the mean time, and what was the central base of operations for the Apache Nation. The first representative to contact her two days before represented the Cherokee tribe of the Cherokee Nation. In light of their complex business dealings around the world, they probably had risk management equivalent to that of the Apache, but for other reasons, of course. Interestingly, Paul Endelphin was also the chief executive officer of the company that designed and produced the Apache Nation surveillance satellites, Syndot. She actually knew him fairly well as a result, and had been on good terms with both him and his company since the surveillance project was first envisioned. The key point here was that she had an equally involved, and almost forgotten on her part, ally in the mess. Her only hope was that his self-serving interests wouldn't tip him out of his own spot on the Council.

As expected due to the Apache and Cherokee joint interests in the current situation, Paul presented her with the full support and assistance of the Cherokee tribe and probably other southeastern Nations if needed to negotiate the current political minefield. The offer was significant, to say the least. The Cherokee tribe was the wealthiest tribe in the wealthiest Nation of the Intertribal Council. Their interests spanned the globe and exceeded most of the other major world powers as well. Businesses held by the Cherokee tribe produced most of the Apache Nation's military equipment and supplies, including those that were held as extremely confidential such as the weapons systems. The resulting collaboration between the Apache and the Cherokee was well known to the other tribes, and possibly envied by some. As she had noted before, she would defend the Cherokee with her life, the reasons being more complex than simple intertribal protection.

Although the Apache Nation had several other strong ties, not all of the tribes felt kindness towards them. Regrettably, they maintained enemies within the Council. The animosity generally remained sub-threshold, but occasionally rose to the surface to cause turmoil in the Council. Prominent among this group was the Pima tribe. Having briefly described the history of the Apache, the problems with the Pima dated back to the Spanish days of the southwest. The Pima had never truly recovered from the effects of Spanish rule and subjugation. A great deal of their tribal identity was swallowed up by the forced civilization, tribute, and Christianization by the Spanish invaders. In the days following the defeat of the Spanish, even at their own hands, the Pima seemed to suffer a great loss. Add this to the Apache's former hostility towards them while they were affiliated with the Spanish, and you had the makings of a centuries old problem that may never be effectively resolved. The General actually believed they would have ultimately preferred Spanish rule to what they had now become, mere shells of their proud Hohokum ancestors. But who was she to say, never having been a member of their tribe.

Another relationship that the Apache had never been able to repair was that with the Comanche. Early on, the Spanish played the Apache against the Comanche in hopes the two tribes would eliminate each other. This deviousness by the Spanish seemed to have caused permanent and irreparable damage to the tribal relationship. In spite of the Apache alliance with the Comanche during both the defeat of the Spanish, and the suppression of the European invasion on the east coast, the two tribes never became true allies. Thinking more deeply about it, the Comanche also had Uto-Aztecan roots like the Pima. In spite of this, she still believed the two tribes' natures were too similar and therefore aversive to an alliance. The Apache and Comanche occasionally had short bouts of cooperation afterwards, but all in all, the problems ran too deep.

This being explained, the most hateful and

derogatory response the General had received to that point came from the Pima representative who also claimed he was acting on behalf of the Comanche representative. She could relate nothing even remotely beneficial from the interaction, and consequently would relate nothing at all. Needless to say, the Apache Nation would continue to protect them because they were part of the Intertribal Council and they had contracts.

The other thirty-plus responses to that point had been a mixture of positive and negative spanning the spectrum between the above extremes. There were many yet to come, and she anticipated a similar ratio of good and bad among them. The political aspects of serving as tribal representative pretty much ruined the job from her perspective.

During the course of the previous few days, Intelligence had sufficiently analyzed a large portion of the current data. With the addition of extra manpower in the form of Cherokee computer analysts provided by Syndot, they had also been able to locate the supposed entrance point used by the hacker. The backdoor had been closed, and Syndot was working to insure the encroachment would never happen again. Apparently, the hacker had been extraordinarily intelligent and sophisticated in his methods. Syndot indicated that only a few hackers known to them in the world were capable of the task, and each was known to work for anyone as long as they were paid well enough. They suggested a clandestine request for similar needs would draw out at least a few of the hackers if the proposed compensation were high and also untraceable. They also agreed to assist in the venture, if it was undertaken.

Intelligence also worked through the crime scene data from the ambush site, and obtained nothing useful. Again, the killer left no trace evidence at the scene. Detailed attempts to pull a facial recognition from the satellite data also failed, mostly due to the killer's supposed mask. Even the efforts to convert extrapolated data from around the mask into a usable face for the recognition software were disastrous, leading even once to a confirmed ID of the killer as Gandhi. As the General noted before, the satellite surveillance had its limitations.

Another interesting piece of information that remained in question involved the spraying of the sergeant's Jaagé with automatic weapon fire. The motive for this was completely unknown. The sergeant had most likely been dead long before the killer arrived at the burial ground. The sergeant's weapon was then left at the site partially buried in sand. Excavation around the weapon prior to its removal for processing revealed nothing of value. The weapon was also found to be functional, and the ammo fired at the vehicle came from that specific Ochnar-75, a compact automatic weapon fitted with a 75 round quick-change clip. The Ochnar-75 was issued routinely to Apache soldiers, and the one at the site had 53 remaining rounds in the clip. After the Jaagé was analyzed for trace evidence, prints, etc., the vehicle was started and operated as if undamaged. This evidence suggested purposeless violence and destruction, aspects that did not fit with the General's previous statements regarding the efficiency of the killer's behavior.

The pieces of the puzzle, and here she literally meant pieces, that she was most interested in were the small squares. The number that was stated earlier had not changed, even after further excavation of the burial grounds by the captain and his team. In addition, none were left at the ambush location. The seventeen pieces had been sent to Intelligence for evaluation, and their presence explained why the General made the trip to El Paso. It was difficult for her to conceal her interest in the little bits of evidence. Basically, they were the only things that had been collected from the killer. Considering his meticulous ability to act without even leaving trace evidence, their existence at the burial ground indicated they were of incredible significance to him.

On first glance, the General understood why the captain had almost overlooked the little things at the burial ground. They were indeed small at approximately half a centimeter in length and width, and were also the color of old bone. The color difference between them and the Sonoran sand at that location was negligible, and would have camouflaged them, particularly if they electrostatically attracted dust particles. Viewing them while they were spread out on blotting paper and under bright lights, she did see a tiny collection of dust surrounding each of the pieces. The squares had not yet been cleaned due to concerns regarding their makeup.

"What are your immediate plans for these?" She asked the tech who basically stood guard over the pieces.

"Well, Sir, I believe the first thing we are going to do is look at them with a low power microscope. We may be able to observe details not visible to the naked eye."

"Excellent, Captain! When do you begin?"

"Right now, General, if that is your order."

"Not particularly an order, Captain. Call it a request."

"Yes, Sir." The captain said smiling.

A few minutes later, the captain had collected a dissecting scope from the storage shelves and attached a video camera to record magnified views of the pieces. Without hesitation, he adjusted the magnification, turned the camera on, and gently slid the blotting paper holding the squares onto the platform of the scope. Pretty unceremonious for such significant evidence, she thought, but then she didn't know exactly what she had expected.

Watching the captain as he slid the blotting paper around on the platform to view each piece individually, she felt a small amount of anxiety gather in her chest.

Abruptly, the captain stood up and said, "I'm sorry, General."

Startled, she stepped back.

"What's wrong?"

"I forgot to hook up a monitor for you to watch while I studied the evidence."

"Oh." she said, feeling a small sense of relief for some reason. While the captain went off to gather the other equipment he needed, she took the opportunity to look at the objects under magnification. After about a minute of staring into the scope, she gave up. All she could see was seventeen dirty little bone colored squares. They all looked more or less the same, with some being dirtier than the others as their only difference.

After this major let down, the captain returned with a cart containing a monitor and cables. He didn't seem to notice her disappointment, so she kept her mouth shut and watched him prepare for her to observe his work.

The first thing she noticed on the monitor was that the objects seemed larger, and therefore she was more likely to catch any useful details. The second thing she noticed was that they still looked like dirty little bone colored squares. Pessimism was one of her strong points.

From a small leather pouch, the captain produced a collection of little tools, and the first of these he used was a very small brush. At that point, he began at the edge of one of the little squares and carefully brushed the surface clean. Unfortunately, the amount of time he spent on cleaning one miniscule fraction of the square's surface proved to be prohibitively slow for the General's attention span. At the rate he was working, the little blocks would be clean in about another month or two.

"Captain, if you identify anything interesting, have me paged."

Lifting his eyes from the scope, the captain nodded his understanding stating, "Yes, Sir," and returned to his work.

She would check back later if she didn't hear anything. Whatever the squares were, they were still high on her list of importance to the investigation. With any luck, they would provide a clue to the killer's identity.

The Intelligence Services Complex was only a small section of the massive Apache Nation military presence in El Paso. This had evolved over time, and she didn't believe it had been originally planned to occur.

As noted in their history, the Apache were

primarily nomadic early in their arrival in the southwest. Even following the creation of the Intertribal Council, the Apache way of life remained relatively unchanged in that respect for some time. The need for their help at various times and in various parts of the Intertribal Council's domain even after the suppression of the Europeans prolonged their wandering, even while some of the other tribes, such as the Navajo, were beginning to settle down and advance their particular ways of life. During that time, the Apache had relatively little to store, nothing in terms of organized training, and no hierarchy of command. Entire extended families remained together as traveling bands, and each band determined its own course of action on an almost day-to-day basis. The bands were not exactly small, however, and they grew quickly as they traveled. Individual bands frequently grew to be the size of independent tribes, but somehow managed to act in unison with other bands during the extended period of conflict.

For reasons unknown to the General, the Apache had previously separated into regional sub-tribes in the southwest that were almost as distinct as the Apache were from the Navajo. At that time, they existed as the Mescalero, Jicarilla, Lipan, Western, Chiracahua, and Kiowa Apache. Over the course of about 175 years, the various Apache bands slowly coalesced into a uniform tribe containing bands from all the major early geographic subdivisions. The accumulation in unified numbers that occurred during these years brought with it a greater need to also establish a home in one primary location. With the gradual stabilization of North America, the Apache were able to filter back into their earlier homelands, the southwest. No longer constantly on the move, they began to develop a more stable military structured similarly to that of the Europeans. This process was accelerated greatly by the knowledge and abilities of the immigrants that had joined with them over the course of their previous nomadic life. As a result, the Apache Nation grew in strength and stability in the El Paso area to become the world-recognized power that it was now.

The General's quarters in the military complex were relatively well furnished even though fairly small. She lived alone, having lost her husband during the Apache's most recent military conflict in what was called the Middle East, a region of southern Asia and northern Africa. The loss was twenty years in the past now, but she guessed she had never really recovered from it.

Over the intervening years, she rose in rank faster than most due to her extensive past combat experience and shrewd decision-making. She was now one of many generals in the Apache Nation's military, most of which were scattered among their bases around the world. She was fortunate to have gotten one of the El Paso postings. Her responsibilities there were fairly light due to both her Council representative status and the relatively low peacetime need of her services. She probably also owed it to the Apache's long-standing interest in keeping families together. Both her son and her daughter were stationed in El Paso now due to their advanced technical knowledge and abilities.

The Apache weapons research facility sat among the already mentioned sections of the military complex in El Paso. In alliance with multiple Cherokee corporations located nearby, the research facility kept some of the best and brightest close to home. Being of high rank, the General was privy to most of the offensive and defensive projects ongoing at any time there. In the previous few years, she had seen the development and production of many wondrous and very deadly devices, the least of which not being the satellite system she had already described. Surveillance, although important, was only a minor component of their global satellite network. The effort and expense of placing a dozen very large satellites into geosynchronous orbit basically put the additional requirement of multitasking ability into the planning process. Their military focus led to the production of massive orbital weapons platforms also capable of surveillance and communications.

When the time for launch came, the Nation

revealed only the communications aspects of the satellites to the greater part of the world, and then, mostly to justify their presence in orbit. There were many other satellites up there, after all, and too much detail tended to alarm the public. Since launch, only the minor functions of the system have been utilized. In a show of great, or possibly misguided, trust, the Nation has never put the weapons systems to test since they were put in orbit. Secrecy, diplomacy and plain old card-up-the-sleeve contingencies also play a part unfortunately.

With the return to her quarters for the first time in over a month, the General had the opportunity to try relaxing for a change. The thought was irrational of course. Whether it was her nomadic Apache blood, or a fear of growing moss on her backside, She hadn't ever been good at 'taking it easy' as some people called it. She thought she must have hit the ground running the day she was born. Today was no exception.

The return to her quarters did, however, avail her of the new technologies added to her system while she was away. High command did have its privileges, particularly when they were duty related. By this, she meant the advanced communications links just installed with instant connect video capabilities. She now had the capacity to immediately contact any base or facility in the Apache Nation no matter where it was in the world and communicate with full visuals. The technology was powered by the satellites and would be useful while she was in her quarters. With the exception of this day, she would probably rarely use this particular setup. She practically never stayed in her quarters. Elsewhere, she did use it almost daily.

Without another thought, she spoke loudly at basically nothing. "Video on. Connect to Intelligence, Lab 14."

Instantly, she had a view of the entire interior of the lab from slightly above eye level. Only two people were already present and working at that hour. Really, the only one she wanted to talk to was Captain Daniels, the tech working on the squares. Fortunately, he was one of the two in the lab, but appeared too busy to notice the large wall screen had lit up with the General's face in its center.

"CAPTAIN DANIELS." She said loudly.

Startled, the captain practically jumped out of his skin, hitting the scope with his hand as he looked up.

"General, I didn't realize you were connected." He responded with a slight flush of embarrassment coming to his face.

Smiling, she recalled his abrupt move that had similarly startled her the day before.

"Have you uncovered anything of interest?"

"Well, Sir, not really. That is unless you're interested in a set of nicely polished, perfectly shaped chips of material that appears to be bone."

"That's it?"

"So far, General. I worked late into the night, and managed to clean eleven completely and carefully examine them. None of them have markings or other features that would particularly distinguish them from each other at this point."

"That doesn't sound good."

"No, Sir, I guess not."

"How can you tell if they're really bone?"

"I'll have to take a microscopic section to absolutely ID the material."

"Is that necessary?"

"Yes, Sir."

"Finish cleaning the other pieces, and I'll check back again later."

"Yes, Sir. What about the section?"

"Hold off for now."

At that, she cut the connection to the lab manually. She still believed the squares, or chips, as the captain called them, were important. She also still had hope that some of them might have identifiable features. Her hope was fading, however, and she suspected the captain would ultimately have to cut one up.

The large wall screen also had a wall-mounted tuner so that it could be used as an entertainment device. Settling into a chair, he decided to watch the world news on the Nationwide News Service. NNS had effectively been developed by the Intertribal Council to provide unbiased coverage of world events. Unbiased was a questionable concept, but in general, the news did capture a large percentage of the major happenings from around the world. Notably, events that could impact the Council or any of the specific tribes were the most frequently and intensely discussed.

The first story or part of a story in this case, focused on the turmoil currently evident in the Intertribal Council. News agencies were not allowed in the Council Chambers, but could wait outside for interviews of the representatives. She hadn't seen any when she left the Chambers, but she was sure there were at least a few in the building. There almost always was. It wouldn't have taken much to get their attention, and the noisy chaos that day probably drew them in like flies.

At that point, several days after the Council meeting, the newsagents were basically trying to get update interviews from the scattered representatives. Few appeared to be talking, but then everybody else may have given interviews shortly after the meeting. She had no idea, because she never watched the news, and they all knew she never talked to reporters. If anything major were currently going on with any of the representatives, the story would still be hot. By the look of this news segment, the topic was already in a downward spiral. The lack of contacts from representatives the day before had also pointed in that direction.

Refocusing her thoughts on the news, the next story immediately caught her attention. With growing horror, she listened to the announcer intently. There had been a murder in the Cherokee Nation's territory. A small boy playing in a wooded area stumbled across the body, and his parents had quickly notified the local authorities. The boy and his parents were all very upset in the interview, and a little difficult to understand. According to the reporter at the scene, the site team had just arrived and was beginning a thorough investigation. A short clip of the interview showed the boy, probably about four or five years old, saying "it don't got no hair". That was all they showed of the boy. The reporter confirmed that she had seen the body briefly, and the hair had apparently been removed. She also believed she had seen bone on the top of the head, but this seemed unlikely to her and was probably a trick of the light. The announcer then came back on, and stated they would show follow-ups as they gathered more information.

There had to be something more to the story to gain immediate attention from NNS. Murder was relatively common throughout the Intertribal domain, and only unusual or sensational cases generally made it onto the Nationwide News Service. Although unconfirmed, her fear was that another scalping had occurred. It seemed possibly over reactive, but it was still the feeling that had crept into her gut. The sergeant's death was eating at her, she decided. She would have to wait on more details, and her current reaction would probably seem ridiculous in the long run.

Leaving the tuner on, the General worked on getting ready to leave her quarters again. It didn't take much effort. She traveled light, and kept what personal items she needed at several of the places she stayed most frequently. The military or the Council generally provided everything else.

While waiting for responses to the Council meeting during her stay there, she had also managed to meet with several local tribal officials from the Apache Nation. They mostly wanted to discuss the issues brought up by the various representative interviewees from the other tribes. What this amounted to was a concern for the financial interests of the tribe. Since a large portion of the Nation's income came as a result of its military, would the breach in security affect the bottom line?

Unlike the militaries of other world powers, a central governing agency such as the Intertribal Council did not control the Apache Nation's military. It functioned on a contract for services basis, and no country in the world was its equal. All of the Intertribal Council Nations paid for their services, as did many of their allies to one extent or another. The Nation's military services were not cheap, but she would have guessed they were far better and less expensive than anything the individual Nations could have provided for themselves. The Apache military were specialized after all, and they dealt almost exclusively in that specialty.

The Apache military focus left other Nations the opportunity to focus their attentions and resources on other important aspects of their own specialized trades. This system would have been impossible to implement in the early days of the Intertribal Council due to the independent natures of each of the tribes. All were used to caring completely for their own needs by whatever means they had each developed, and trust was clearly a major issue. But centuries of intertribal peace along with constant mingling of the tribes had generated trust in the Apache's abilities as well as their honor. The other tribes had basically learned that the Apache would not take advantage of their military might and had cultivated their own aptitudes into successful means to support their people.

As a result of the security breach, the tribes of the Intertribal Council had reason to worry about the Apache's abilities. They alone stood watch and protected the others' interests. Should the other Nations change decades of near single minded focus on other things, or continue to contract for Apache services?

To the General, the answer to them all was fairly simple. There was no way they could develop effective militaries in the short term due to a long list of reasons. Generating and maintaining a military was expensive, very expensive. Training soldiers took time, and a fairly established and rigorous system. Development of new military oriented technologies was also costly, and required a certain expertise in fields that were otherwise of minimum use. Diversion of manpower and other resources would detract from their current interests. This would reduce their financial ability to both sustain a military, and more importantly, survive. Other, less important factors also came to her mind, but the major points were significant enough to calm the local leaders. She believed also that the other tribes in the Council had come to similar realizations over the previous few days. Ultimately, nothing would change.

What still bothered the General was the possibility that aspects of the sergeant's murder had been engineered to cause turmoil in the Intertribal Council. Infighting in the Council, a sign of broader intertribal hostility, could potentially bring an end to centuries of relative intertribal peace. Like the continued and centuries old problems the Apache had with the Pima and the Comanche, most other tribes had their own intertribal issues. Some of these conflicts flared up to be newsworthy at times, and took little provocation. As an adjunct to their usual duties, the Apache military had assisted local militias several times in maintaining the peace. It generally never got that far, but agitants arose in almost all societies at one time or another and the current one was no exception.

Of course, the scalping and sacred ground violations that caused her to call for the Council meeting should have worked in the opposite direction and led to greater unity. When the meeting had been initially called, she felt a sense of universal fury from the other representatives. They had all, in their not so distant pasts, suffered similar atrocities. Had she not revealed the satellite breach, the outrage would have continued towards the outside where it justifiably should have remained. But that took her back to second-guessing... What was done was done... She had shown continued honor and respect for the other tribes by her revelations. In the long run, she had to remember that fact.

An hour and thirty minutes later she decided to call the local law enforcement agency covering the new murder in the Cherokee Nation. She hadn't seen anything new reported by NNS, other than their usual speculative bullshit. Although a long shot, her gut told her she had to assess the situation anyway. Ignoring gut feelings usually led to regrets, and she had enough of those to keep her occupied for a while.

CHAPTER 5

Following several hours of nonsense, the General's contacts in the Cherokee Tribal Police were finally able to get accurate details on the Cherokee Nation murder. Apparently, too many of them relied on NNS for their current events, and the story on the News Service had gone from horrifying to preposterous within hours of the initial report. Per the last report on NNS, the deceased had been hunting and shot a rabbit. By the time he reached the rabbit, a pair of turkey vultures had descended on it. In the man's attempts to get his rabbit, he had been attacked and mauled by the vultures, leading to his death and the loss of all of his hair. Had she relied on NNS, she would still be in El Paso. As it was, she now stood in the basement morgue of Cherokee Tribal Police Substation 72 waiting to view the body.

The Cherokee Nation was dramatically different from the Apache Nation in many ways. Geographically, the Apache were stuck way out in the desert, a harsh and inhospitable place even in the best of times. They had drifted into that location on their own, and had even chosen to go back when the Intertribal Council ultimately brought the tribes peace. They could, of course, go anywhere now, but they still mostly chose to stay in the desert.

The Cherokee, on the other hand, had apparently drifted into the southeast from the northeast, the area where most of the Iroquoian-speaking natives had remained. The heart of the Cherokee Nation's domain, the lower Appalachian Mountains, was heavily forested to this day, and lumber was a minor business of the Nation. As noted previously, the Cherokee were very business and technology oriented.

The Cherokee also had initial contact with

Europeans by intrusion of the Spanish in the 1500s, but were apparently less affected by them, unlike some of their neighboring tribes. The later arrival of the English proved a different matter. The English established numerous colonies on the east coast, and gradually worked their way to the interior and the Cherokee. Trade with the Cherokee quickly developed, and they acquired goods, including guns, that greatly changed their way of life. Unfortunately, the English encouraged most of the tribes they encountered to capture enemy natives and trade them as slaves. The Cherokee were no exception to this, and were soon trading in and being taken as slaves themselves. As such, conflict among the tribes was encouraged tremendously beyond its preinvasion level, and an early reduction in the number of natives began to occur purely through the process of war.

At the same time in the east, the Europeans brought numerous diseases with them that many of the natives had never experienced. Small pox was the worst for them, and their numbers were reduced somewhat by their lower immunity on initial contact. But while these things were occurring, extensive business dealings with the Europeans also resulted in intermarriages with the Cherokee and other natives. These unions generally saved the tribes involved by imparting greater immunity to illnesses in the following generations. Even so, a few eastern tribes were completely decimated by the diseases the invaders brought very early in the invasion, whereas the invaders themselves and an assortment of the tribes managed to survive because they carried the immunity from their dark distant pasts.

The local Cherokee Nation medical examiner, Dr. Albert Desoto, was a seasoned professional who had seen many horrible things in his life. Calmly waiting for his assistant to collect the body, he pulled on gloves and prepared his tools for the autopsy. Just another routine exam he imagined. The Apache General's presence was a little unusual, but there was no accounting for individual tastes when it came to using free time.

"General Cochise, have you been present for

many autopsies?" He asked.

"I've seen a few, doctor. Most of the carnage I've seen was on the battlefield though. Cause of death was pretty much irrelevant most of the time."

"Understandable. Well, this shouldn't be any different from what you've seen in the past, in terms of autopsies I mean. I'll go through my usual routine. If you have any questions, just speak up."

"Thanks, doctor."

The first thing the General noticed as the gurney rolled in was the blood-specked skull. No mistakes could be made in that observation. Having recently seen the same on Sergeant O'Connor, she believed she was less shaken than the doctor. She would have ventured a guess that he had gone his entire career without seeing a single scalped head.

"Scalped." She said in a matter of fact way that brought the doctor's head abruptly turning in her direction.

The doctor, showing an incomprehensible level of surprise, nodded.

"I guess this is why you're here, general?"

"Well, yes, partly. This does provide confirmation on one of my concerns." She answered unshaken. The doctor was already recovering from his shock.

"What else do you need to know?" He asked, now calmly settling into his routine.

"Mostly cause of death from you now doctor, but other things in the long run."

Nodding again, the doctor turned on his overhead microphone with the foot switch, and quickly began to recite observed details. After the description of the scalping in medical terms, the General watched and half listened until he came to the description of the massive contusion on the body's upper chest. The simple fact that it was there and of a similar nature to that found on Sergeant O'Connor brought her one step closer to what she ultimately expected to be the cause of death. The pathologist would probably have no idea what she expected him to find considering his reaction to the scalping, but he may have had contacts associated with the Council. The idea was extremely unlikely, but still possible she thought. In no mood to prolong the autopsy, she kept quiet, and let the medical examiner continue his exam.

A few minutes after the doctor made his Y-incision, the General watched as he used a bone saw to cut through the ribs. He soon documented medial and lateral fractures of the left fourth and fifth ribs, as well as apparent punctures of the left lung and the heart's right ventricle by the flail rib segment. Blood had pooled and coagulated in the pericardial sac following the cardiac rupture. Aside from the horrible evidence of the scalping, the murder had been extremely tidy and self-contained. The killer should get a prize, she thought. She would be happy to deliver it in person.

Having seen what she needed to see, she thanked the doctor and bowed out before he could ask her any questions. The details matched what had been reported of the crime scene. The lack of blood at the scene had been attributed to the body having been dumped, which was still partially true. Since the body had been dumped, there was no evidence of a struggle at the scene. Thorough processing of the scene had, so far, produced no evidence. The site where the murder occurred had not yet been identified, and there were no witnesses coming forward at this point.

The General's initial gut feeling about the NNS story had been correct. The entire situation was now unfortunately familiar and a clear pattern was forming. After all, hitting someone in the chest hard enough to produce heart damage and death was an unusual form of murder. She had confirmed this with multiple sources. In addition, the chest injuries appeared to be caused by a similar or probably the same blunt object. This placed the killer into a fairly narrow set based on manner of death and weapon choice. Since there was a pattern emerging, a scan of any of the available world crime databases should reveal any previous deaths approximating these unusual criteria.

What remained to be determined in the new case was the identity of the victim. The local police were working on this now. With that available,

scans of the Apache Nation's military databases
could reveal if any linkage to the first murder was
present, and could also lead to a possible motive
for the new death. She didn't have a lot of hope
for this. Death following these injuries was
undoubtedly slow, allowing the killer to torment
the victim by scalping them while they were still
alive and aware. This indicated the work of a
pretty sadistic killer who probably had little need
for motives beyond pure sociopathy. The pattern
also suggested a serial killer was roaming the
Nations, something rarely reported in the
Intertribal domain but relatively common elsewhere
in the world. NNS reported the capture of such
people all over the planet on a near regular basis.
Whether these reports were all accurate was
impossible to tell considering the slant NNS tended
to take in their current reporting. She did
believe, however, that similar cases in the
Intertribal domain would not escape the NNS, and
therefore, were unlikely to exist. Of course, the
NNS had attributed this death to turkey vultures,
so assuming that any of their stories had a solid
foundation in fact would be foolhardy at best.

At that point, three other pieces of data were
available to the General, but not to any of the
investigators locally. First, she would not have
satellite images of the body being dumped. She had
requested and obtained the satellite data on
arrival in the Cherokee Nation. Review of the data
for the body dump coordinates had revealed
beautiful aerial views of the surrounding woodlands
that rarely if ever penetrated to ground level.
She had expected that after seeing the story on
NNS, but it didn't make her feel any better. The
major weaknesses in the Apache surveillance system
would have to be resolved, and she didn't mean the
hacker incursion.

Second, review of historical records for the
general area there provided no clue of why the body
would have been left in its particular dumpsite.
The site held no known significance to anyone in
any way. Sergeant O'Connor's body, on the other
hand, had been placed on sacred grounds, and the
grounds had been further disturbed by the killer's

placement of the squares in the sand.

Finally, the site processing team there had not found a single similar little square under the body. Naturally, they wouldn't have known they should be looking for anything buried in the soil below the body, but any sign of disturbance below the body should have clued them in. She believed this was particularly true for woodland soil, unless of course the killer had been meticulous about replacing the dirt, leaves, sticks and whatever else was on the ground before he disturbed the soil. Considering what she knew of him so far, she guessed it was a reasonable possibility. She would have to go to the site herself and check the ground. The General also thought opening her hand at that point to reveal what she already knew by involving others would only open the door to further Council hostility. At least, that was her well thought out rationalization.

With nothing else to do in the Knoxville area since she had gone there for only one purpose, she got into her Jaagé and headed slowly for the coordinates where she knew the body had been found. The currently calculated delay of over thirty hours since the locals' initial site processing would probably leave the scene empty and ready for her own search. What she planned to do when she got to the location would pretty much destroy the integrity of the site, and would also generate tremendous hostility from the local officials if they returned and found her out there. She would just have to take that chance.

During the drive, her mind drifted to the Council's eventual lack of a sustained reaction to the first murder. Amazingly, it was never mentioned in any of the many discussions she had with other Council representatives after the emergency Council meeting. She still found it surprising considering the reaction she got when she first requested the meeting. Apparently, Apache security breaches were far more unbearable than scalpings and sacred ground violations. It was an indication of their continued slide from their heritage into the reality of modern times she decided.

With her attention on the recent past, she
forgot to purchase digging tools, and reached the
dumpsite with little to work with. Of note, she
also lacked her characteristic gut reaction for
things she should, or in this case, shouldn't do.
She decided she would have to improvise on both of
them.

Rationally, the absence of her gut feeling was
in essence a sign in itself... Tools would
definitely be an easier thing to improvise.

A normal speed drive by followed by a creeping
return put her a little at ease regarding being out
there unannounced. It was too bad it wasn't also
insurance against anyone returning. But she had to
do this, she told herself over and over. She was
the only one who could if she wanted to keep the
buried squares under wraps.

Finally, armed with the only reasonable tool
she could find, the Jaagés jack handle, she
approached the site with continued caution.
Nothing had been left behind to indicate what had
happened there, not even crime scene tape. Her
worries about stirring up local law enforcement had
clearly been a waste. If not for the GPS in her
watch, she would have been digging for a couple of
years and probably then in the wrong spot.
Fortunately, she had input the coordinates into the
GPS memory when she requested the satellite video,
and now could pull it up and locate the exact spot
the body had been left.

After identifying the proper location, the
General meticulously cleared a six-foot square area
of all of its leaves and other forest debris with
the coordinates at the center. A lengthy
inspection revealed that nothing lay immediately
beneath the debris. It was lucky for her because
if it had, even the worst crime scene technician on
the planet would have already picked it up and
carted it off. Considering this, she quickly got
back to work. The ground was extremely soft and
easy to manipulate. It would take her little
effort to make it as far as a foot down if she
found it necessary. She didn't really expect to
have to dig that deep, but she would go down two or
three feet if she had to in her effort to find the

squares.

A little while later, she had gathered the soft first half-inch layer into a small pile near one of her cleared corners. She hadn't noticed anything remarkable when she scraped up the soil, but she hand sifted it into another pile several times anyway just to be sure. It was too important to her to be sloppy, but even then she still found nothing. Careful but impatient and a little disappointed, she moved on to the second layer. In this layer, she picked up a few worms and small stones very quickly, but careful sifting again revealed nothing particularly interesting. More frustrated now, she went back to her first layer of soil and checked it one more time. She then returned to the second layer's pile of dirt, but after another slow round of sifting, she didn't find anything in the second pile. Feeling more disappointed but also reasonably sure of her results, she decided to take a short break. Her lower back was starting to ache and since she was in this for the long haul, she also needed to stretch her legs for a while.

Walking slowly back to the Jaagé as she attempted to stretch the pain away, she tried to recall exactly what Captain Atwell had told her about his own excavation. She had no idea how deep he had found the squares, but she could only imagine that they had been extremely shallow, considering the way the killer had quickly and almost casually swept the sand. There was also a major difference in soil types between the two places obviously, and this could reasonably have affected the way the killer would be able to leave any buried objects. She just had to reign in her impatience and keep working the site. But as much as her back was aching, three feet down was starting to seem pretty unreasonable for her, not that she had ever seriously considered digging that deep in the first place.

Shifting her attention from her back, she looked around the general area and instantly lost hope that the murder location would ever be found. The area was so densely wooded that there appeared to be no reasonable way to even begin a thorough and productive search. This probably contributed to the reason the whole crime scene area had already been completely abandoned. In the absence of an eyewitness or a miraculously lucky break, the local authorities probably had about as much as they would ever get on this killing. The idea was somehow even more disheartening and quickly took her back to where she had been digging.

With very little extra effort, she went down an inch and a half on her next pass. Nothing appeared any different than the first two layers until she came nearer to the center of the dig. At that point she felt the jack handle scrape over what would most likely be another rock to add to her growing pile of pebbles. Somewhat irritated by the prospect of carefully sifting out even more useless junk, she continued scraping towards the center. Her first annoyance was rapidly followed by several others, all of them giving off a similar stone against metal clink. Approaching her limit for tolerable irritation, she decided to stop and sift for junk before she had even scraped half of her area. When her quick, half-hearted sifting of the partial layer yielded nothing, she decided to look for rocks or other debris protruding from the ground. The jack handle had clinked against something. With the irritation progressing even further towards frustration, she had an abrupt urge to give up on her clearly useless effort. The little squares under the sergeant's body had probably been a fluke, she thought to herself. They could have been there hundreds, even thousands of years for all they knew, and they didn't even know what the hell the squares were!

Angrily standing up without regard for her back, she grabbed the jack handle and pulled it back towards her. With this effort, she both heard and felt the handle scrape across something hard in the soil. She was sure she had felt the little clinks this time, her senses possibly enhanced by her growing anger. Running the handle back over the same area repeatedly produced the same clinking vibrations, so she stooped down and stuck her face as close to the soil as she could without eating dirt. At the right angle she could barely make out

a few tiny ridges in the dirt. Catching the edge
of one with her fingernail, she tried to work it
out of the soil, but split the nail instead. Now
using the jack handle, she found it edged the ridge
easily out of the ground. With a combined sense of
relief and excitement, she realized she had her
first dirt covered little square from the dig.
Carefully inspecting it, there was no mistaking its
similarity to the ones Captain Atwell had found in
the desert. Totally forgetting her prior back
pain, she returned to excavating with a zeal she
never thought she could muster for a patch of dirt.
It wasn't a quick process, but every square she
unearthed brought another surge of adrenaline, and
before long she completely lost track of time and
her wooded surroundings. When she eventually
stopped making direct recoveries from the
excavation, she began to resift the soil from the
evidence layer as well as all of the ones above and
below it repeatedly until she was satisfied she had
gotten all of the squares. As darkness settled in,
she collected what little she had and headed toward
the Jaagé with the jack handle and her squares.
Once there, a brief attempt to view the squares
with the dome light revealed nothing more to her
than a pile of chunky dirt, and she pulled away
from the site to head back to Knoxville.
Pessimistic as she was, she still managed to feel
happy and satisfied with her finds and her slowly
developing set of conclusions.

With her unexpected exhilaration, she felt an
unusual urge to celebrate her find. It would be
stupid and a pure waste of time, but it wasn't
every day that she found the virtual needle in a
haystack. In all likelihood, she probably never
would again.

The only person she even marginally knew in
the area was the Cherokee Council representative
Paul Endelphin. His local office and primary home
were supposed to be in Knoxville from what he had
said in passing before. They could at least get
something to eat. As she neared Knoxville, her
previous thought turned into resolve and she
attempted to contact him via the Jaagé's satellite
link. He would have a link in his office. Well,

he probably had hundreds of links scattered throughout his holdings.

As she hit the outskirts of Knoxville, she activated her voice-controlled link and attempted to connect to his office. After multiple attempts to secure the link, she was kicked into his messaging system so she ended the link. Another attempt to reach him, this time at his home, brought a member of his household staff on to the link to inform her Mr. Endelphin was currently out of town and most likely could not be reached at the moment. With a brisk "thank you", she terminated the link and realized she had already burned through a big chunk of her exhilaration.

Her stay in the Cherokee Nation ended shortly after she learned Paul Endelphin was away on business and when she had also retrieved what little new information she could from the locals about the Cherokee Nation's victim. Within a few hours, she was back on a jet heading for El Paso, and had more than her share of questions still to answer. Fortunately, she wouldn't have any down time since the plane was also equipped with satellite-linked communications. After a brief call to her Council office to check on the status of the recent disturbance, she put in a call to Lab 14. The link system continuing to operate perfectly, she quickly had a direct video link into the lab, and again had nearly startled Captain Daniels out of his skin.

With the last ebbs of her exhilaration, she struggled to hold in a smile and said, "Captain Daniels, you're in really early again today."

"Yes, General, couldn't sleep." He said, realizing she had just seen him shoot nearly a foot off the ground.

"That I can understand. Must be all that adrenaline pumping through your system." She said humorously before asking "What's your status with the evidence?"

"Well, Sir, I finished the cleaning, and other than what you already know, I can say I have nothing new to report."

"So they're all featureless, I assume."

"Yes, Sir. At least at the magnification I

65

have been able to study them."

Still feeling a need for some solid answers, she asked, "What do you think, Captain. What are they? Do you have any idea?"

He quickly answered, "Sir, I believe they're all made of the same material, possibly bone. They're almost identical in size. Otherwise, I don't know, Sir."

Pausing and then accepting the limits of what he could discover superficially, she asked, "Do you still think a section would reveal what they're made of?"

Again without hesitation, he answered, "Most likely, Sir."

"You can proceed with the section then. I also want you to be prepared to evaluate another set similar to the ones you already have."

With a blank look, he asked, "What do you mean, Sir?"

"I'll show you when I get there. Get to work on the section." She replied.

"Yes, Sir." The captain nodded, obviously confused by the mention of 'another set'.

Settling back in her seat, she pulled the small packet of new evidence out of her jacket pocket. The little squares were about the same size as the first set, she thought. They were quite a bit darker in color, but she could see in some places that they were still a dull shade of white beneath all the forest grime. She suspected the darker white could have been a result of the rich woodland soil they had been buried in. Like the first set, the blocks appeared to be made of some very tough material, since her efforts to dig them out of the soil with the jack handle hadn't damaged them as far as she could tell. They were most likely made of bone as she suspected the first set was following her report from the captain. There was one difference between the two finds. All together, she managed to get eighteen squares from her site. Even after double and triple checks, she had found no more and had accepted that the eighteen were all she would ever find. Following her own painstakingly obsessive search, she now wandered if Captain Atwell could report the same about his own excavation. He and his team had found one less piece than she had, and if the number eighteen was significant, there was still a block buried at the desert site. She could be pretty sure she hadn't picked up a look-alike. All eighteen pieces were planted thin edge up and to the same depth as if they had been deliberately driven into the ground with some strange tool. The precision by which they were placed was very different from the random scatter that the desert blocks had been found in. She could imagine even this had some possible significance to the killer. Something she might find out before she killed the bastard.

The remainder of her flight was uneventful. Her Council office had reported no new activity regarding the Council meeting. The situation had completely cooled down, and it appeared that everything was back to business as usual. That would undoubtedly change when word of the most recent scalping murder got around. In spite of the wild story coughed out by NNS, the truth would leak out sooner or later. This time, she hoped the focus would stay where it belonged, on the horrendous murder and the monstrous killer who was bold and crazy enough to be scalping the Nation's people. Unfortunately, she knew better.

CHAPTER 6

General Cochise's arrival back in El Paso was heralded by news that there had been another major earthquake near Mexico City while she was in the air. That made two in the past seven years, and little had actually survived the first with it having been a magnitude 8.7. The Apache Nation facilities in El Paso had been rudely shaken from a distance, but were built to withstand a magnitude 10, if such a disaster ever happened to hit El Paso directly. However, Mexico City was probably flattened again. It would be less of a loss this time around, since anyone who didn't absolutely have to return didn't go back to risk another quake after the last one. The past quake had killed well over a hundred thousand people, and the damages had been in the billions. When she put these figures into perspective, she saw part of the reason the former Aztec capital had missed out on the Council Building-South site. She still harbored a feeling that the quick and easy Aztec conquest by the Spanish played a big part in the decision though, and would still probably never know the whole truth no matter how long she sat on the Council.

Needless to say, the Apache Nation would be sending a large quantity of aid to the local tribes. She had nothing to do with the relief efforts directly when it came to the Apache Nation's military, but would still be doing a fair amount in that area as a Council representative over the course of time. Although the Spanish had overly influenced the majority of the southern tribes in the 1500s by force, Spain had little to nothing to do with them now. In fact, Spain had dwindled into the shadows of world power, and could no longer be recognized as the land that had produced the world-roving conquistadors. There was a small amount of justice in that from the General's perspective. The near total decimation of multiple native cultures on their initial arrival should have had a higher cost for the Spanish. She would venture so far as to set the penalty as their inability to continue existing on the planet. But then, she was an Apache warrior and they didn't hold grudges, they settled them permanently.

What she had planned to be a quick stop by her quarters to change clothes and prepare for another unexpected trip to the Western Council Building turned into a major delay. As nearly uninhabited as they were, her quarters had been broken into while she was away. To her, this was like breaking into a bank vault to steal stagnant air. She kept nothing there of any value, whereas the rest of the Apache military complex would be a virtual goldmine to anyone in the know. A brief search later, and she had confirmed that all of her worthless stuff was still with her, even though some of it had been tossed around a bit. She was just about to connect to Complex Security when she realized the communications system had been left on since she left her quarters three days before. Since her system was preset to automatically shut down if there was no activity for three hours, she knew she hadn't personally forgotten and left it running. The stupid thief wasn't as stupid as she had initially thought. The burglar had been seeking access, not property, and had undoubtedly gotten all that he wanted.

Using a landline, she contacted Security without touching her system. They would sweep for prints when they arrived, and then she could do a back run and see what had been accessed from her terminal. Unfortunately, she never utilized the security features in her system. She was in her own Nation and in the middle of the whole damn Apache Military Complex to boot. She could never have imagined anyone would break in to use her access. But considering the recent hack into the Apache satellite system, she should have taken precautions. Her terminal allowed unquestioned access to a large percentage of the Complex's systems as well as to the Council and numerous Cherokee corporations. The breach was purely her fault. That is if she disregarded the duties of the entire Security department. She had enough to worry about without blaming herself for another general security breach. If the Apache wanted to maintain their position in the world, they were going to have to tighten up their ship. She knew this for certain without even knowing the severity of the current breach.

Complex security arrived minutes later, and her place was scoured for remnants of the intruder. With the exception of the crew that had upgraded her communication system recently, no one had been in her quarters besides her in almost two years. After all, it was small, and she was never there. Her kids were used to a transient military life, and this was definitely not 'home' for them. Besides, they were all Apache. The closest thing to a home they had was the southwest, the whole southwest.

After dusting for prints, Security's digital

detectors scanned the prints that were found directly into the Nation's database, and quickly spit out the expected. She had been in and all over her own quarters. The only other prints found were those of the communications crew, and they were isolated to the area of the Com station. The intruder had more or less trashed her place without leaving a print, unless he was a member of the Nation's communications crew. Even then, he would have needed to trash her place while wearing gloves, and then could have taken them off to use the terminal. Pretty unlikely, but she would have it checked out. Also, the system was still on when she came into her quarters, so the intruder had been in and out within three hours of her own arrival as determined by her own auto shutoff settings.

As expected, the crew was ruled out easily after a short call to Communications Systems. Based on their duty rosters, they were all on the other side of the Complex, and all present and accounted for during the past three hours. Her hope now rested predominantly on the results of a back run. For privacy reasons, it being an officer's quarters building, there was no camera monitoring of the hallway outside of her quarters. Even though they were all Apache and would not steal from one another, she had always felt this was a stupid oversight. After all, she had nothing to hide, but then she must have been in the minority or else the hallway would have been monitored. Maybe the breach would change things.

Two hours later, the Security team cleared out, and she had an opportunity to do her back run. As previously noted, she had access to a great deal of very confidential domain, and the Security team, thorough as it had been after the fact, was no longer suitable company. She could manage on her own now, and needed to just based on her own levels of access. Pulling up the accessed data history screen, she stared briefly at the small print, and decided she needed a cup of coffee to get through the rest of the day. With the murder investigations, the Council problems, and now the earthquake and her security breach, she didn't plan

on sleeping for at least another thirty hours, and
that would be a pretty good caffeine driven run for
her age.

While making coffee, she tried to assemble her
thoughts into something approaching order. In the
past week, she had suddenly collected a lot more to
think about than usual, and as noted before, she
always kept busy anyway. The overload could
eventually mean she would have to delegate some of
her worries to other people. At that point, she
didn't feel comfortable with delegating anything.
She was too heavily invested in all of her efforts,
and would have to waste a lot of time just bringing
someone else up to speed.

Her principle duty would still have to be to
the Council. She really had no way to delegate any
of that responsibility, so would have to deal with
all of the Council related earthquake issues
directly. Most of the work would be political,
making the appropriate tribal contacts and
reassuring the representative's that Apache aid
would be available. Her staff could work out the
details beyond that and she could request any
further assistance she needed from the Nation. The
new crisis would also place the previous Council
problems on the back burner, and allow her to focus
on the murders and security breaches.

The security breach with the satellite had
already been dealt with whether the other Nations
were aware of it or not. The General's new breach
was a different story, and had to come second on
her list of responsibilities. She could delegate
part of this to Security, but not anything
involving confidential matters. This would push
the murders into the bottom slot on her agenda, and
she really wanted them to have more priority. Her
interest in the scalping murders had gone well
beyond her desire to seek vengeance for Sergeant
O'Connor. The murders were becoming a very
intriguing mystery that she felt compelled to
solve. In fact, even though she could leave the
entire investigation to a long list of appropriate
authorities, she couldn't see herself relinquishing
it to anyone. She would just have to go longer
without sleep.

Before she could get back to her search, she received a call from Security. The outer doors of the Officer's Quarters Building required an authorized pass card be inserted to allow entrance. The officers used their military IDs for this, and a log was generated showing who had used the various doors over the course of time. On reviewing the building access logs, Security had found what appeared to be a sick joke on somebody's part. Several hours earlier that day, and in fact, within the time frame that her quarters were broken into, a sergeant had attempted to gain entry into the officers' quarters by way of a pass card. Sergeants were not housed in the building and did not have access, so the door had not opened. But the sergeant's attempt still registered in the log. Security found the log entry unusual because the sergeant had recently been flagged as deceased.

Placing the phone back in the cradle and settling back into her chair, she tried to account for what she had just heard. Security was absolutely right in their description of the failed entry. It had been a sick joke or maybe even something worse. The attempted entry had been by way of Sergeant Ilya O'Connor's ID, a task she was clearly no longer capable of performing.

The General's mind flashed through the possible culprits in this failed building entry. She had not yet thoroughly reviewed the interview files developed when the sergeant's family had been contacted. Really, the only thing she knew regarding those contacts had to do with their fields of work (since she had been focusing on retaliation at the time). She suspected there would be information in the files concerning the sergeant's past and more recent relationships, as well as what the family had observed about these relationships. It was unlikely that anyone in the Apache military had tried to use the ID. The Apache were all aware of the entry restrictions coded into their IDs and also into the security systems. In fact, she wasn't even allowed direct entry into a large number of buildings in the facility. She could, of course, seek permission, but it would still be a one-time thing not coded into her ID, unless her duties required frequent readmissions. In this particular case, she logically had to believe that the user of the ID had no knowledge of the carefully observed entry system.

The General's back run would take less than a second, but could provide extremely valuable information including giving her a list of each and every file and system accessed since the com station had been updated. This was a new addition to the abilities of the individual com stations, and one she had thought pretty useless until then. She hadn't been able to imagine why she would want to look back through her own com activities, particularly since she would rarely be there to use the system in the first place. She had been wrong, and she was happy about it for a change.

Shuffling through the multitude of options in the system to find what she wanted took at least 45 minutes. They could have made the system more user friendly, but then maybe it was for people who had actually been trained to use it. Another thing she had thought useless until then, and her irritation with the system indicated she was no longer happy about being wrong. There was always a balance to life, or at least there had been to her's. Unfortunately, her balance tended to favor the negatives a little bit more than the positives most of the time.

Eventually she got to the part that would only take a second, selected the option, and sat back to take a look at the results. She waited a lot longer than a second, and nothing came up. Thinking that she had probably hit the wrong option by mistake, she reselected it, and again sat back to view what her com station had been up to while she had been gone. Knowing that she had definitely selected the right option this time, the blank screen was kind of unsettling. Since she had used the system the last time she was there, something should have come up. But no matter how many times she selected the back run option, the log came up totally empty. The supposedly tamper proof log had either been erased, or just plain didn't work. To quickly test the system, she clicked through

several local connections, and pulled up another
back run. This one contained every link she had
just made even though each had only lasted a
fraction of a second. The damn log had been erased
clean! She still had no idea what the intruder had
been after and would possibly never know.

The General got up and started pacing back and
forth across her quarters, her mind racing through
countless disturbing possibilities. Of course,
none of her thoughts on the matter were good, and
she finally had to sit back down just to calm down
a little bit. The coffee kept her heart pumping at
a rapid but steady rate anyway, and the two worst
things that had repeatedly raced through her head
just wouldn't go away. Considering her current
concerns, she suspected either someone from the
Council, or even worse, the killer had been there.
The probability of either being capable of getting
into the complex, past security, and then in to her
own personal quarters was infinitely small, and yet
someone had done the virtually impossible and
gotten in. As heavily armed and well trained as
she was, a chill still ran down her spine.
Whatever was going on, it had become personal. Not
having a clue to the intruder's identity or
motives, she gathered up the few things she would
need for her next Council trip, and cleared out.

Although most of the Council site's tribal
representatives had returned home or proceeded with
their pre-emergency Council meeting projects, a
select few had remained at Pueblo Bonito. Whether
as a result of paranoia, or just their combined
reasonable distrust of the Apache, an alliance had
been formed over the years. Not surprisingly, most
of the alliance consisted of tribal representatives
from Nations surrounding the Apache Nation, the
Pima and Comanche representatives being the most
avid throughout the course of the long-standing
pact. Many other tribes had drifted in and out of
the alliance over the years, mostly in response to
what they viewed as transgressions by the Apache.
But the two tribes at the heart of the alliance had
stood firm, and shared an almost single minded
enmity for the Nation that sat directly between

them. John Clandridge, with 37 years of service to the Council, sat as the senior member of the pact and held his position as proudly as he held his Council seat. Most of the alliance members who had stayed at Pueblo Bonito over the past week now sat in his office as they had been doing daily.

Having just completed his summary of the extremely small amount of useful intelligence his Nation had gathered over the past few days, Steven Headrinne of the Shoshone Tribe waited for questions.

"Do you think your team will come up with anything else now?" John asked, sensing the progressively increasing level of disappointment in the room.

All of the other representatives turned expectantly to Headrinne, but his brief headshake and "No" was followed by a prolonged silence in the room.

Edward Parker, the Comanche tribe's Council representative, sat quietly waiting for the next alliance member to detail his Nation's contribution to the very slowly growing data packet the alliance had gathered over the week on the new situation with the Apache. As the silence spilled beyond ten minutes, he abruptly stood and left the room. They weren't getting anywhere. All they had managed to come up with in an entire week was validation of Cochise's report to the Council. It was becoming irritatingly clear that the Apache Nation had not only presented the truth, but had openly provided damning evidence of their faults, and it seemed most of the data available to them at the time as Cochise had stated. He had wasted an entire week here on the assumption that the alliance would dredge up more than a few discrepancies or better yet outright fabrications and lies regarding the recent events. What they had now was suitable for open conversation on a tapped, public telephone line in the center of the Apache Nation.

Slipping quickly into his own offices, Parker waited patiently for John Clandridge to come to him. They had developed a habit of analyzing things in a little more detail than they felt comfortable with in the presence of the other, more

transient alliance members. The Pima-Comanche pact
was carved in stone, and the two trusted each other
as much as two people of different tribes and
Nations could manage on an 'enemy of my enemy is my
friend' basis. Of course, eleven years together on
the Council also helped. That, and the fact that
neither of them had stabbed the other in the back
up to that point, even though they had passed
through some relatively tough times over those
years.

After waiting far longer for Clandridge than
he appreciated, Parker poured two shots of Shawnee
whiskey and sat down behind his large, ornate desk.
When his fellow representatives were onto something
really important or more likely than that just
shooting the shit, they were all true politicians
and could blab on for hours. Having left seven
alliance members behind not including Clandridge,
he might as well accept reality and settle in for a
longer wait. He had already blown a week, what was
another few hours at this point.

Parker's thoughts drifted back home to his
massive, and very profitable ranch in the Comanche
Nation. What had begun as an extreme affinity for
horse breeding in the early days of the Comanche
had progressed to large scale and broad spectrum
breeding of almost all forms of livestock
imaginable. The Comanche had acquired land within
most of the Nations, and now raised whatever
livestock was most suitable for the particular
climate where they had purchased the land. The
Comanche Nation had become as wealthy and powerful
as the Cherokee and Apache Nations, but by
different means and the means suited them
perfectly.

In what seemed a necessity during a period of
serious stagnation in his past, Parker had also
delved deeply into the Cherokee realm of science
and technology. With his and a few others'
unprecedented successes, many of his tribe followed
and the Comanche Nation as a whole now owned the
largest and most advanced animal genetics labs in
the country. Their productivity had increased
dramatically as a result of the new technology, and
they had become the largest supplier of animal

protein on the planet. The once barely struggling to survive handful of Comanche bands had become wealthy beyond imagination, and their closest tribal brothers, the Shoshoni, had benefited as well. Taking all of this into consideration, the current issues with the Apache were pretty meaningless to the Comanche Nation. Their interests were dramatically different and they even relied significantly on each other's services now. The much weaker Pima Nation and its cohorts might have more serious concerns, but the growing Comanche wealth served as a massive buffer within the Nations and in the world as a whole. Their wealth allowed them to purchase protection beyond the basic Intercouncil services of the best military available, and that just happened to be the Apache. In spite of age-old differences, the Comanche and Apache interests in the world had gradually merged, and he and most of his Nation's people currently held no true animosity towards their Apache neighbors. In fact, on a purely business level they had become staunch allies that were bound tighter than the Comanche in their long pact with the Pima. Clandridge, in his lifelong self-absorbed vendetta against the Apache, had failed to recognize the changes that were actually quickly taking place around him. The Comanche Nation's interest in the outdated anti-Apache alliance had only continued to exist in blind allegiance to their age old and also outdated pact with the Pima Nation. If he ended up wasting even another day of his very precious time on this nonsense, he might have to make some dramatic and unexpected changes in the Comanche's Council position regarding the Apache. His wealth had recently been about the only thing that had kept him in his position as the Comanche Council representative. Most of his Comanche brothers and sisters had been steadily heading towards dissolution of the pact or at least a Comanche Nation withdrawal for several years, and they had a growing financial backbone to support them that he could no longer ignore.

As Parker swallowed his second shot of Shawnee whiskey, he continued to wait. His patience

wearing thin, he had a strong urge to contact
Cochise right then and bridge the gap that his
Nation had been encouraging him to overcome for at
least a year now. His long held, and apparently
misguided friendship with Clandridge had seemingly
run its course. All he had left to do was lower
the hammer on the old man.

As if he had sensed Parker's thoughts,
Clandridge knocked and came through his door
without waiting for an invitation. He appeared to
be in a pretty good mood for someone who had also
just wasted an entire week of his time chasing his
tail at Pueblo Bonito.

"What do you think?" Clandridge asked as he
took a seat across from Parker.

"What do you mean, what do I think?" Parker
returned without a second's hesitation.

Continuing to smile, Clandridge settled deeper
into his chair. "What do you think about the new
data, of course? Looks like were really getting
somewhere now."

Looking at Clandridge in obvious confusion,
Parker leaned forward on his desk and asked,
"Weren't you just at the same meeting I was, John?"

Chuckling a little bit and completely missing
Parker's real meaning, Clandridge responded, "Good
one wasn't it? Lots of new and important
information."

Sitting back in his chair, Parker asked, "Did
something spectacular happen after I left? I
didn't hear anything worthwhile when I was there."

John Clandridge's smile quickly faded as he
stared at Parker, now actually trying his best to
comprehend where Parker was coming from. The other
representatives at the meeting had given him
extremely positive feedback when it was over, and
he had felt greatly encouraged by the meeting
himself.

"Well, no.." He said, "but our information is
still building, and I think we're on to something
big."

"And what would that something big be, John,
complete confirmation of the Apache Nation's self
incriminating credibility in all of this? That's
the only path I see us walking down right now, and

I've just wasted a week of my time in the process."

Seriously taken aback, Clandridge was momentarily speechless as he tried desperately to envision where Parker had jumped the tracks. They had been friends for many years now, and he had grown to trust their likeminded view of the Apache threat. A confused look slowly crept over Clandridge's face as he continued to have difficulty coming up with anything worth saying.

Again leaning forward and resting his elbows on his desk, Parker broke the silence. "John, we've known each other a long time, and this is difficult for me to say to you now, but only because we've been friends for a while. Most of my Nation has been pushing me to ally with the Apache for at least a year now. Hell, we use their special security services and have for quite awhile. The Comanche Nation basically trusts the Apaches enough at this point that we have placed a great deal of our assets and our lives into their very capable hands, and they've done a damn good job with it all so far. I guess what I'm really trying to say here John is that my tribe and my Nation are done with the alliance at this point, and considering the time I've now wasted this week, I finally and logically have to fully agree."

Parker looked more closely at Clandridge. If he hadn't known better, he would have sworn that the old man had just been shot short range in the chest with a muzzleloader by his very own mother. His jaw had dropped completely open, and he had gone so pale that it looked like he was on the verge of bleeding out. He remained speechless for several minutes, and Parker seriously began to wonder if he had just witnessed the old man having a massive stroke. Clandridge definitely wasn't taking this well…

As the General made her way across the massive Apache military complex on foot, she continued to dwell on the unexpected and bizarre intrusion into her quarters. It was only with a very deliberate effort that she managed to shift her thinking to the positive, and wonder if Captain Daniels in Lab 14 had some new data by then. He should at least

have the results of the section he had taken, and
that alone might be of considerable help. She
didn't know what other plans he was developing for
the squares, but she was beginning to feel the
urgent need to give him permission to do whatever
he thought might be necessary, even if it led to
the eventual destruction of the evidence. The
killer was leaving the squares for some reason,
either as a message to them, or for some other less
obvious but equally significant purpose.

Finally arriving at Lab 14, she quickly
entered and headed immediately for the Captain's
workstation. He appeared to be extremely busy as
usual, and she watched for a few minutes to see
what he was doing. When he eventually glanced up
at her, he did a double take, and then snapped
almost comically to attention.

"General, Sir."

Continuing to look at what he had been working
on, she quickly said, "At ease," and followed with
a friendly "How are things going?"

Relaxing only slightly, he looked back down at
his work, and answered, "Well, Sir, Right now I'm
still working at cleaning the new bunch of squares
you brought in so that I can better compare them to
each other and also to the first set of squares."

"Did you get the results of the section?" She
asked expectantly.

Unceremoniously, he said "Yes, Sir. The
section was definitely bone, and was further
identified as human."

Checking another mental box in her assessment
of the murder, the General looked back down at all
of the little squares on the viewing platform.
From where she stood, the new squares that had
already been cleaned looked identical to the
original set. Taking another step in reasoning,
she decided that her new found squares hadn't been
in the rich and moist Cherokee Nation soil for very
long or they would probably have stained and
appeared slightly different in color from the
others. She would have to take a closer look
through the scope to make a more accurate
comparison of the two sets. Just as she was
starting to move even closer to the workstation,

the captain switched on the monitor he had hooked up for her before, and several of the first and second sets of squares abruptly appeared on the screen and greatly enlarged. She still couldn't see any difference in coloration between the two sets. Superficially, they were all the same in size, shape, color, and apparently material makeup as well. They were going to have to get a more detailed analysis to get any further in the investigation of the squares.

"Captain, you have my permission to take a section from each of the squares for comparison."

"Yes, Sir. I'll get right on it." He said seriously.

She would now have to wait again for results, so she made her way to the lab's small vending lounge and bought a cold bottled coffee. The caffeine content rapidly brought her thinking into better focus, so she sat down in one of the lab chairs to work out her next steps in the investigation. She didn't have much time before she would have to head back to Pueblo Bonito for the next scheduled Council meeting. She needed to decide whether she should present the Cherokee Nation killing to the Council, or hold the information back until she could possibly have a better understanding of the significance of the squares. She didn't feel she could even consider revealing the existence of the squares until she had a vague idea of what they signified to the killer. At least that was what she now kept telling herself as she thought about the Council and the various factions that would quickly attack if they thought she didn't have a good grasp of the investigation. She had been pretty bold in revealing the initial information to the Council, but it was time to be more cautious, much more cautious.

CHAPTER 7

At the wooded edge of a recently plowed field, a Shawnee Nation farmer saw a dark mass of unusual movement, and quickly slipped off of his still running tractor to investigate. He had heard reports about a pack of wild dogs roaming the local area, and they might have even been wolf mix. Gripping the well-used 12 gauge he had been carrying with him for that very reason, he moved cautiously toward the dark restless mass, and held his breath as he crept close enough to hear low-pitched growling that was way too close for comfort. The dogs abruptly saw him, and all seven turned to assess whether their next target was predator or prey. Before he had a chance to even raise the shotgun, the dogs had made their assessments in unison and were starting to form a tight circle around him. Four of them were medium sized, but there were three of the seven that definitely could have been part wolf. Feeling his time running out, the farmer jerked the shotgun up and blasted birdshot into the sky. The animals flinched a little and then slowly backed off a few feet as he pumped the next shell into the chamber. With the pitiful reaction the first shot had gotten, he took no chances and fired the next into the freshly turned earth at their feet. A scattering of pellets hit the two dogs that were now closest to him, and they all leapt frantically into the woods at their back and were too far away before he could level another shot. Now shaking violently, he took a dozen deep breaths and scanned as far into the woods as he could for several minutes before he dared to move forward and take a closer look at what they had been violently working on. He didn't know what he had imagined, but he definitely hadn't expected what he found, and he immediately went back to his tractor and tried to contact his farm on the tractor's radio, hoping there would be someone around to answer. When he eventually got a crackling response from the radio, he managed to tell his wife to send the local authorities out, and to have their son lead them to the field if necessary. He would move his tractor over and guard the partially mauled human body in case the dogs were brave or hungry enough to come back for more.

Parker's sickening fear that Clandridge had

suffered a stroke right in front of him fortunately didn't bear out, but he would still be stuck at his Council offices for a while longer preparing for the upcoming Council meeting. Clandridge eventually composed his pasty faced self and with the attitude that he had been repeatedly slapped in the face, stormed out of Parker's office without another word. Parker knew there would be little if anything left between them now, but that only meant there had also been nothing beyond the supposed Apache threat holding their friendship together in the first place. Even if Clandridge refused to or just couldn't see it, the world was changing constantly, and you either adapted the best you could or apparently in Clandridge's case came pretty damn close to having a stroke.

With his duties on the Council now directed solely in the direction desired by his own people, he felt a considerable amount of relief settle in that he truly hadn't anticipated. Smiling, he poured another shot of whiskey, and sipped it slowly as he thought about the next moves he should make for his Nation. He was completely representing the Comanche Nation's best interests again, and now free and clear to do whatever he needed to without being bogged down by century old and now irrelevant feuds. His first overture would clearly have to be toward the Apache Nation, and he had to determine the best way to proceed down a path that had always been absolutely barricaded to him. There was still a little time to figure his next move out, but now a full year of intense effort at Pueblo Bonito suddenly didn't feel like enough time to prepare for what would most likely be an earth shattering shift in the political dynamics of the Western and possibly even the entire Intertribal Council. He could call his two closest advisors, but they thought like he did so the decisions would still ultimately be up to him. He just needed to buckle down and use what skills he had to work it out.

General Cochise stared at the monitor again as the captain placed the next section on the stage of the high-powered microscope. After several hours,

he had managed to determine that every section and
therefore every square checked up to that point was
composed of human bone. He had actually only
managed to get through six of the squares, but had
been delayed somewhat by the need to clean a couple
of the squares before he could section them.
Feeling relatively confident that all of the
squares from the initial set were the same, he had
moved immediately on to sectioning the second set
of squares to provide the General with a quick
burst of previously unknown information. The
General hadn't thought to ask him to do it that way
since she had been dwelling on other things at the
time, but was happy with his thoughtful
organization of the whole process. He had also
planned out the next required step in the analysis
from his perspective. He couldn't actually do this
part of the analysis himself, but it would provide
them with a potentially vast amount of otherwise
unobtainable information. He just had to determine
where to have that part of the analysis done, since
the Apache Nation didn't have any labs specializing
in that particular area of bioscience. He would
have to investigate the options available to them,
and he wasn't even sure yet if the technology would
be accessible to them from any of the other Nations
that they routinely collaborated with on the
Council.

     With the knowledge that the squares from both
murder sites were made of human bone, the General
had nailed down another solid link between the two
horrendous crimes. It would now be quite a while
before she had the next round of data, and with her
caffeine boost dwindling, her ability to
concentrate on the investigation was starting to
fade down as well. Glancing at the wall clock, she
noticed the giant monitor positioned on the wall
next to it, and walked across the lab to power it
up with an NNS feed. She could still deal with a
passive flow of information, even though she was
starting to get really tired. With the touch of a
button the monitor popped brilliantly to life and
she tuned quickly to NNS. The tail end of the
weather showed clear skies over both El Paso and
Pueblo Bonito at the moment, and then the image

shifted to a calm and average looking newscaster sitting behind a desk with the NNS logo plastered across the front. The man instantly went into a droning report of the major events occurring in each of the Council's Nations, as well as the world as a whole. Moving to the most comfortable chair she could find in the lab, a dark leather lounger, she settled back and quickly had to fight sleep to keep track of the newscaster's monotone voice. He definitely wasn't going to help her stay awake, and she thought of getting another cold coffee to pull her up. But before she could register the thought seriously enough to actually start moving, she slipped into what became a dead tired sleep, her body's attempt at recovery from her week of pushing herself too hard due to the investigation.

Less than two hours later, she struggled to wake up in response to someone calling her name. But she wasn't ready to be awake, and kept falling back asleep within a second of hearing her name. The captain eventually lightly touched her arm to try to help her wake up, and realized his mistake the instant her fist plowed into his groin. Falling to the ground and gasping for breath, he lost focus for a minute, but she quickly hauled him staggeringly to his feet. He made a mental note as he finally managed to recover his breathing, vision and balance at about the same time; the General was a hell of a lot stronger than she looked, and he had never considered her a light weight.

"Captain… Captain, are you all right." He thought he heard as he slowly processed his last thought. The next thing he knew, the leather lounge chair was swallowing him up as the General pushed him off of his still unsteady feet.

"I think so, Sir…." He said quietly, thinking at the same time that he wasn't. He felt like he was going to throw up his last six meals.

As the General turned to look around for a water fountain, the image on the wall monitor caught her attention. The NNS feed was still on, but the scene of a farm field somewhere had replaced the droning newscaster, the sunlight already weakening behind the tree line at the field's edge. The words BREAKING NEWS scrolled

laterally across the screen as she observed a swarm
of people surrounding something on the ground at
their feet. In spite of all the possibilities, she
had a horrible déjà vu gut feeling that this story
was relevant. Of course, she also heard the
captain in the background trying to direct her
attention to the monitor, and the realization that
he had been trying to wake her up to see the story
clicked into her mind along with a little bit of
sympathy for him. She sincerely hoped he already
had as many kids as he wanted. She knew how hard
she hit because she had nearly killed her husband
once when he startled her awake like the captain
had just done. A smile crept onto her face as she
remembered, then quickly slipped away as she also
remembered that her husband was now dead. She
would have to make it up to the captain when this
was all over, she thought. It would be a
reasonable thing to do under the circumstances.

Still watching the monitor, the story seemed
to jump back a little ways. NNS was probably
running a film loop to reduce their labor costs.
They were pretty good at it in a blatantly obvious
way, and it seemed to be effective at the moment
since she got to catch the beginning of the story
without having to wait forever. There was a first
time for everything, she thought as the voiceover
kicked into full gear with details of what was
currently known at the scene, or at least currently
when the loop was recorded.

The disembodied voice reported, "..at the
location of a partially decomposed body found by a
local farmer. The farmer here in the Shawnee
Nation midway between St. Louis and Louisville had
just finished plowing the field, and noticed some
strange movement in this area. The farmer has
indicated he had to drive away a pack of scavenging
wild dogs with a few blasts from his shotgun. Then
he realized what the dogs had been eating, and
immediately contacted the local authorities. The
Shawnee Nation's crime scene investigation unit was
immediately dispatched and is currently
investigating the scene…."

Without a second thought, she used the closest
control unit to switch the feed to a Shawnee Nation

news network, knowing the biased and often ridiculous twist NNS had developed in its reports over the past several years. The new program manager had apparently worked a great deal in the tabloid television arena before moving up to his current NNS job. The network was now more fluff and fantasy than hard facts, and it was getting difficult to even watch the NNS version of the news.

The image on the monitor barely seemed to change as the feed switched to the new report. The press was confined to a limited area, and the camera work looked nearly identical to NNS. The live local reporter had already been doing some serious investigative work, however, and her report was vastly different from the heavily filtered NNS version the General had already heard. BREAKING NEWS wasn't scrolling across the picture either, and the difference in the view was striking. She could clearly see a body on the ground surrounded by the investigators, and the body was nothing short of human. The lighting also put an incredible shine on the top of the bare skull, and the General's anger welled up briefly as she added a third possible body to the killers list. The Council meeting would have to wait. She had to get to that Shawnee Nation field and do a thorough search that she knew only Captain Atwell and herself would know how to do at that point. She would drag Atwell along with her to do the dirty work since he seemed to have far less trouble dealing with the dead than she did. Her arrival there would also cause a stir, and she needed Atwell to work the scene while she played politics with the Shawnee Council representative as well as the local authorities and investigative units if necessary. Apache Generals who were also Council members didn't appear in the middle of nowhere without a really good reason. She was going to the vastness of nowhere and would have to contrive a reasonable purpose, or risk having her investigation splashed all over NNS.

George Rand, the Shawnee Tribe's representative to the Intertribal Council sat in

his artifact filled Eastern Intertribal Council
Building office at Cahokia, sifting through
newspapers to get a better understanding of the
current world around him. NNS only scraped the
surface of the news, but the written press managed
to cut to the bone every time. He knew for a fact
that there was far more information available in
print than would ever hit an NNS news feed.
Knowing this made all the difference. He had
already come across the farm field body story in a
whole stack of papers, and each one seemed to have
an extra detail or two not present in the others.
The Shawnee Nation had an incredible infusion of
German ancestry dating back hundreds of years, and
the Germans were detail oriented. He trusted his
people to reveal the truth just as Tecumseh had
revealed the truth to his Nation during the latter
days of the hostile European invasion. Rand and
his Shawnee Nation relied on themselves and the
truth above all else. He could envision no other
Nation in the Intertribal Council that could stand
by such a maxim as truth, honesty, and reliability.
He was proud to call himself Shawnee.

    Swiveling away from his desk full of the day's
newspapers, George looked out his expansive wall of
glass to see the Cahokia ruins stretching out
before him. The Ancients in the area had been what
they now called the Mississippians, temple mound
builders with a culture that had rivaled any on the
continent at the time, or for centuries after.
They were the most advanced early eastern American
civilization, and their culture pulled from other
even earlier cultures in the Mississippi river
system including the Adena, Hopewell, and possibly
even the earlier Poverty Point culture. They had
lived well, and apparently prospered in their time,
their massive earthen remnants lasting to the
present day as evidence of their ingenuity.

    As he looked at the well-formed earthen mounds
left behind by the Mississippians, the farm field
body pictures from the papers returned to his
thoughts as a harsh reminder of human nature. From
the information he had gathered in the dozens of
local papers, the person's death had not been
accidental. First of all, there were so many

fractured ribs visible around the sternum through animal ravaged skin that the person could possibly have died from blunt force trauma to the chest, or at least that was what the local experts had indicated in their preliminary findings. The second disturbing feature was the lack of hair on the top of the skull. The newspapers indicated that there were marks on the skull of some kind that corresponded with the missing hair, and could possibly point to an abomination in the eyes of the Intertribal Council along with anyone who even had the slightest shred of decency. Just from the preliminary data at that point in the investigation there was a suggestion, unbelievable as it may have been, that the victim had been scalped, sending the person's soul into a tormented and damned afterlife with the soul doomed to walk the earth in agony, never able to rest and never able to go beyond as all souls must. Mutilation of the dead was an act of extreme hatred and was deliberately intended to horrify the living and bring an eternity of misery onto the dead. There would be no return for either party involved in such an insult. The act was purely evil in every sense of the word.

George continued to stare out over the Cahokian ruins bad thought followed by bad thought. He couldn't comprehend anyone so evil as to be capable of such a thing. Turning back to his desk, he reached for the control to turn on his wall monitor and realized the teleconference light was slowly flashing above the screen. Someone was attempting to connect to his system. Much like the old-fashioned phone services, if he didn't pick up the connection, it would just continue to attempt to link indefinitely more or less informing the caller that 'no one home'. He had requested deactivation of the video mail feature with the expectation that people would keep trying to reach him until they actually did. It was probably irritating to some of the people on the other end, but he held to the probably outdated belief that if it was really important they would keep trying. Few people did unless it was to complain about something. The world just wasn't the same as it had been when he first joined the Council.

With the touch of an also flashing button, the monitor kicked to life revealing the image of a uniformed woman, high ranking by the amount of rank bands across her moderately endowed chest. He wouldn't have noticed her chest without the rank bands, or at least that's what he thought to himself blushing slightly. He was too damned old to be having those kinds of thoughts.

"Council member Rand?" the woman asked immediately, without giving him a chance to compose himself. The old phone system had been more anonymous, and he missed it now that the Council had forced him to accept the new technology.

"Yes. How can I help you?" he responded almost on reflex.

The woman didn't hesitate.

"I'm Council member Cochise of the Apache tribe. I'm glad that I was able to reach you."

Recognizing her instantly from the recent emergency meeting, he responded flatly," I know who you are, General. Again, how can I help you?"

"It's an honor to speak to you, Council member Rand of Tecumseh's Shawnee tribe." She said with what appeared to be sincere respect.

She had already polished her diplomatic veneer, he thought, recalling that she was relatively new to the Intertribal Council. He couldn't imagine an Apache general being quite so polite otherwise. Not that he disliked her, or her tribe. The Apache had provided significant assistance to the Shawnee even before Tecumseh's day, and the invaders would possibly have prevailed if not for them and the fledgling Intertribal Council. General Cochise had suitably honored him by the mere mention of Tecumseh's name. She was already an adept, and it would prove useful to remember that in the future. In this and other things, his accurate recall of history had always served him well.

"It is an honor to speak to you directly as well, Council member Cochise." He replied, finally composing himself, and realizing the reason for her call at the same time.

She hastily went on, "I'm calling to request your permission to enter your Nation in service of both of our tribes, as well as the Council as a whole."

Pausing briefly for effect, he took a closer look at her, and realized she was not only a little shaken below the formal facade, but also clearly exhausted beyond anything he had experienced even at his age. The dark circles under her pale blue eyes severely aging the face that could have been on one of his descendents, he imagined, estimating her age to be around fifty.

"Is there a connection between the murder in your Nation and the one I have been reading about in mine?' he asked, rhetorical questions a mainstay of his diplomatic interactions with other Council members.

Not taking offense to his pretended ignorance, the General went on without hesitation. "In strictest confidence, and honor of the dead, I can tell you that I believe so."

Pausing again, he made a deeper assessment of her sincerity. Direct contact by another Council member was a rarity. Beyond that, political contact from a tribe outside of the Cahokia region had been nonexistent during his time on the Council. The oldest member of the Council by far, he knew his history. The situation was dire, and he felt compelled to give his full cooperation.

"I see. And have there been others."

Hesitating momentarily to calculate her ability to trust the ancient man at the other end of the teleconference, she nodded and said, "One that I am aware of." From her experience, it was difficult to trust anyone other than her own tribe, and outside of her direct command, it could often be difficult to do even that.

Sensing the extreme leap of faith she had just taken, his resolve solidified, and he calmly answered, "With Apache Nation bases already strewn across the Shawnee Nation, you need not request my approval. Your conduct is well noted, however, and my Nation will give you its full cooperation."

Breaking the connection, the General slumped a little in her chair. The bog of political crap that accompanied Council work was almost more than

91

she could tolerate. Why she had accepted this
appointment remained a pathetic mystery in her
mind. Tip toeing through bureaucratic bullshit was
beyond her training, and the steep learning curve
she continued to negotiate dug at her military
sensibilities like sandpaper on road rash.
Politicians were a different breed. Whatever band,
tribe, or Nation they had evolved from didn't come
from this planet, or at least, not from anything
human and dwelling on the surface. The mythical
nightmares of the spirit world crept into her mind,
and she shuddered like a small child hearing her
first ghost story in the intermittent darkness of a
stormy night. If not for the serious and now
personal nature of her investigation, she wouldn't
bow to this nonsense. It wasn't the Apache way, or
even the way of any of her European ancestors fit
enough to survive the rigors of the Americas' past.

CHAPTER 8
        After landing at the Apache military base near
St. Louis, Sioux Nation, the General loaded into a
Jaagé that had been left for her and Captain Atwell
along the runway. The Apache Nation's military had
bases in the Shawnee Nation they could have landed
at, but the St. Louis base was the closest to
Cahokia, and they would diplomatically have to stop
through there before heading to the site where the
body was found. Since she had already made an
introductory and very polite appeal to the Shawnee
representative to the Council, she was fairly
positive that the political delay would be brief,
and they would be on their way quickly, or at least
that was what she anticipated before they arrived
at the Cahokia Intertribal Council Complex an hour
and a half later. Unfortunately, Council member
Rand had some very different ideas about the
General's stopover. A small delegation of
representatives from various Eastern tribes met
them in the lobby of the main Council building when
they walked in. She recognized a few of them from
the holographic projections at the Pueblo Bonito
Council Chambers, but she recognized and actually

knew only one Council member besides George Rand.

"Council member Cochise, it is good to finally meet with you in person here at Cahokia!" the Cherokee representative said as he beat the other representatives to her by a fraction of a second. Paul Endelphin, looking younger by decades than most of the other Council representatives, shook her hand happily and with true sincerity.

"I'm sorry you're here under these circumstances, but it is an honor to have you at the Eastern Intertribal Council site all the same." He said graciously. "I'm also sorry I missed you when you were in my Nation recently. I will have to make it up to you."

Soaking up what Paul Endelphin had just said, the General's thoughts were rudely interrupted by George Rand as he slid quickly up between them with more speed and energy than she would have ever imagined him capable of, and grasped her hand in a vise like grip almost before Paul Endelphin had let go of it. Already startled, the strength of Rand's grip surprised her as well, and she immediately added these factors to her overall assessment of the ancient man. Beyond that, he looked even older in person than he had in either the hologram or on the link, and she guessed he had to be near a hundred years old if he was a day. Rand's bloodlines had to be beyond extraordinary, she thought as she smiled and nodded to the two of them.

"Council members Rand and Endelphin, I'm happy to be here even during these grim times." She said, the smile remaining only as a formality. Her thoughts were still almost fully elsewhere, and she felt a significant delay in the making as more Council representatives came forward to introduce themselves and shake her hand. She had difficulty maintaining the smile during the barrage, and the various representatives' names and tribal affiliations didn't fare any better in her memory. She did manage to keep count for some stupid reason, and the number eventually climbed to twenty-four before she finished shaking hands. Before she could say a single word in protest, she was being herded towards what she knew would be a large meeting room just off of the lobby. She had been to the same one in her own Intertribal Council building more times than she could count.

When everyone had settled into seats around the massive conference table in the center of the room, George Rand, of all people, remained standing. In her irritation with the delay, she decided he looked more like a magically animated skin covered skeleton than anything else, and as she gawked he continued to defy the laws of humankind, and pace energetically back and forth at one end of the conference table. The sight was so disturbingly eye-catching that she had difficulty shifting her focus to the others at the table.

Still pacing, he began to speak, and immediately had the attention of everyone else in the room. "As I managed to tell each of you who had not read it in the papers or had not seen it on the news before General Cochise arrived, we have a very disturbing pattern developing among the Nations, and I believe it deserves our immediate attention."

Looking around the room, the General realized that her once discrete and personal investigation no longer fit into either of these preferred categories. The small bubble she had been caught up in popped silently but with a disturbing amount of force. What had she expected anyway, to track the killer down single-handedly and extract her vengeance on the monster privately? The situation had grown well beyond herself and the Apache tribe now. If the new found body in the Shawnee Nation field fit the pattern, they now had three murders spanning three distinct Nations, and the outrage should reasonably engulf the entire Intertribal Council, if not the world.

Looking at the other people around the table, a few of the faces brought a faint remembrance of a tribal affiliation back to her mind. The recognition had to be from the holographic images of prior Council meetings, because the rapid introductions a little while before had definitely not registered solidly in her memory. Directly across the table from her sat Council members Jones of the Mohawk tribe and Thick of the Huron tribe, both of the Iroquois Nation, and two of the people sitting between the General and the pacing animated corpse-like figure of George Rand. Sitting next to the two Iroquois Nation representatives, the representative of the Chickasaw tribe also appeared to be mesmerized by the puppet-like movements of Shawnee representative Rand. She must be new to the Council in this region, the General thought. That, or Rand's appearance and behavior were unusual for him. Thinking about it twice, she was absolutely sure the Chickasaw representative was new to the Council. Rand was ancient, and she fancifully briefly postulated that he was somehow a Mississippian still living at his centuries long home of Cahokia. She mentally chuckled to herself. Even a long dead and desperate to return spirit wouldn't inhabit that hideous old body. This idea bringing her thoughts back to the dead, the body found in the Shawnee field resurfaced vividly in her thoughts, and the time she was currently wasting began to weigh heavily on her gut like a big fatty meal. There had better be some meat to this meeting, she thought or she was going to get up and walk out, the hell with diplomacy. Again, she acknowledged that she wasn't cut out for this part of being a Council member, and returned to watching Rand. How could she not?

"Council members," he said, "we have a crisis on our hands. Following the mutilation described by Council member Cochise in the emergency meeting recently, a similarly disfigured body has been found in the Shawnee Nation. I was extremely alarmed by this when I read about it. My concern magnified beyond any normal comprehension when representative Endelphin of the Cherokee tribe and Nation today informed me that the body found in my Nation was not the second, but the third that had recently been mutilated in a similar manner."

The room rumbled with loudly whispered conversation as the significance of what Rand had said sank in to the gathered representatives' minds. Aside from the Apache victim, there were now two victims from the Eastern Division of the Council. The unlikely nature of the crimes, considering the punishment dealt out by every tribe

95

in the Council, warranted a massive investigation beyond anything the Council had ever needed to pursue. The implications were astounding. A murderous force was attacking the strongest alliance in the world, and doing it indiscriminately. At that point, horrendous offenses had been perpetrated without a single clue as to who had done them and why they were done. Following an apparent golden age of the Intertribal Council, someone had the nerve and the whereabouts to rattle the Council to the bone. The room gradually died down, and the Shawnee representative went on.

"My Nation….and I have taken the liberty to grant this without conferring with the other tribes in the Shawnee Nation….is going to cooperate in this investigation to its fullest extent. We are under attack! We should spare nothing to resolve this, and have no mercy when the perpetrators are captured."

The rumble in the room turned into a raucous response of agreement. Rand had accomplished his goal, and the General again felt that she had a set and personal mission to accomplish. Standing, she looked at Rand, and nodded her approval. He was still extremely capable, and her recent thoughts brought a little guilt. She would do her best to track down the monster that was terrorizing the people, and eliminate him. Her resolve was again firm.

Thanking the gathered representatives, she quickly took the opportunity to escape. The political quagmire had cleared faster than she could have ever expected, and she was again on her way to examine a mutilated corpse. It wasn't exactly rational, but she felt a sense of relief, and more importantly, renewed purpose. Her investigation would proceed and most likely dos so without interference, at least in the domain of the Eastern division of the council.

The General was quickly out the door, Atwell tailing her as soon as she left the conference room. She was now thinking that if they hurried, they could make it to the body before nightfall.

Captain Daniels had been able to finish the sections from all the squares just before the General took off, and was now working on the details of the necessary continuation of the analysis. All of the pieces had been identified as human bone. If there was any connection to be found between all of the squares his first thought was that the most likely useful scientific determination would be genetic. A genetic analysis could reveal a multitude of facts that were far beyond his level of training. Sometimes it wasn't what you were capable of, but what you could delegate to the appropriate capable party. In this case, he would definitely have to go beyond the Apache Nation. Although now a member of the Apache Nation, he had been born Comanche. Greatly against his family's wishes, he had decided that he aspired to a military life, and had sought out the Apache Nation. The Apaches had readily accepted him, in spite of the centuries old differences between the Comanche and Apache, and he had been absorbed as if he were a long lost sibling. There were no second thoughts. He was now of the Apache Nation, and proud to be where he was. As with most of the individuals within each of the tribes and Nations in the Intertribal Council, however, he had solid and undeniable links to his ancestors. His ancestors were from the Comanche tribe, and had been master geneticists for centuries, although initially at a crude level of course. His biological siblings still resided and worked in the Comanche or probably any other Nation, and were affiliated with the most advanced molecular biology corporations in the Comanche Nation. He knew where he needed to go to get the analysis done, and he would have to contact the General to get approval before he jumped across the political Apache-Comanche chasm that lay before him like the Grand Canyon. They needed the best for their analysis, and there were no better than the Comanche when it came to genetics. There were no better in the entire world to his knowledge.

Mentally preparing himself to present his case to the General, he walked to the com station and dialed out to attempt a connection with her satellite link. The General carried a data card that could be plugged in to any of the Nation's Com Stations throughout the world. Her link was therefore portable, and the Satellites would locate and connect to her like a paging device when anyone was trying to contact her. All she had to do was plug the card into a com station to open the video link. Since all of the Apache military vehicles had small in dash Stations, the captain would be in contact with the General immediately, or at least that was what he anticipated. The attempted connection pinged repeatedly, but the General didn't pop up on the wall monitor. He allowed the pinging to continue for several minutes, but there was no response. He would have to keep his resolve up, and try again a little later.

The time leading up to the next Council meeting kept Edward Parker fairly busy as he researched and carefully milled through anything he could find on General Cochise, and the current global status of the Apache Nation. There was surprisingly little available on either subject, other than the usually shallow and self-serving press releases that every Nation put out occasionally, including his own. Most of what he could find, he already knew because of his association with Clandridge. John had an obvious obsession with the Apache Nation, and hoarded any and all information about it, factual or not. Obsessed people could be very dangerous from Parker's experience, obsessions often falling outside the realm of rational behavior. Clandridge fit that bill without question, and the thought of him hounding away after the Apache for all of these years was now a little unsettling. Parker's move away from the anti-Apache alliance would make him fair game for Clandridge and his pact. They hadn't ever done anything drastic, but the potential was definitely there and he knew John would use anything he had to his advantage without regard for the truth or who he might damage in the process. As he took a short break from reading, he sat back and looked at the meager page of notes he had accumulated over the past several hours.

Unfortunately, he had more information already
stamped firmly into his memory. Putting the piece
of paper back down, he pulled what he already knew
to the forefront of his thoughts. Unfortunately,
most of the information about the Apache Nation was
military in nature, and therefore classified. What
was clear from the outside, however, was that they
had the most advanced and powerful military on the
planet, and had ventured as far as Luna and Mars
with their military space program. They used their
technology and warrior skills to protect a large
portion of the world from the rest of the world
that didn't or couldn't pay them. If you could
afford it and you paid them well, the Apache
protected you with their own lives. They were
basically mercenaries for hire, and gained the most
financially by providing protection services to
various Nations across the world, including his
own. Of course, they would protect even extremely
vile people who could fork out the cash and do so
even if there were conflicting interests with
others they also protected. This part he had never
been able to get a good grasp on, but they managed
it somehow and profited greatly from it. Most of
the Intertribal Nations utilized their services. In
addition, the technology rich Nations like the
Cherokee collaborated with them to increase their
military power and therefore their ability to
protect the whole. In spite of the benefits, the
efforts by all of the associated Nations were
minimally altruistic. They all had their eyes on
the infinite potential beyond earth. The Comanche
Nation could reap incredible benefits by embracing
the Apache. He could initiate this with a little
carefully directed effort, and he planned to do so
even if it took more than just a little effort on
his and his Nation's part.

General Cochise's history was a little more
open to public scrutiny, partly because of her
heritage, but mostly because she had never
attempted to shelter herself from the media even if
she wouldn't talk to them. In short, she was
honorable and therefore had nothing to hide. At
five feet ten inches, she was relatively tall for a
woman, and had jet-black hair. She was physically

well conditioned, and had a well proportioned body as a result. In addition, she had the most advanced combat training available, and had served in several wars with minimal loss of her troops. The General had been married, but lost her military husband to the most recent war. She had two children from this marriage, both of whom served in the Apache Nation military like their parents. Both of her children remained unmarried at this point, and she had no grandchildren. In view of everything available, her life had been gradually heading toward the political arena long before she had been selected for the Council. Her focus had become her roles in the military and the Council, and she probably had little time for anything else.

Parker had only seen the General at the Western Council site, and then she had always been in the standard military uniform of her Nation. Of course, it was a little more ornate than the uniform of the average Apache soldier. The details came with rank, and there were few in her Nation if any that she could be viewed as subordinate to. Add Council representative to the picture, and she was one of the most powerful people on Earth. Based on all of his knowledge, she would make an incredibly good ally. Currently unmarried himself, he could envision many directions a friendly relationship could go with her, allies on the Council not the least of these. He would and could put out an incredible effort to secure her friendship. It was clearly the next logical step in his plans.

Shortly after his first failed attempt to reach the General, Captain Daniels pulled up a link with her traveling in her Jaagé. In the passenger seat, she calmly stared at the screen as the surrounding countryside flew by on either side of the image he had on the giant wall monitor. Her driver had to be pushing them as fast as the Jaagé would go, and that was pretty damn fast. The military version of the Cherokee Jaagé had an engine that almost overpowered the chassis, but then the vehicle was light and built for speed even in the consumer model. He had one himself, and there was never a lack of power.

"Captain" she said without a change in her demeanor.

"Yes, General, Sir. I have been assessing our options for the analysis of the squares, and we do not have the appropriate facilities within our Nation." The captain started.

Feeling an intense pressure for time as she rocketed down the highway, the General abruptly cut the captain off before he could present his options.

"Captain, do whatever you feel is necessary." And she shut off her monitor.

The captain stood stunned for a second, and then felt a wave of relief since he didn't need to argue his point. The weight of the situation settled on him before the relief had pushed away the stress. It was his decision, and in spite of his strong feelings about who would do the best analysis, he didn't know what to do. This was worse than what he had been preparing himself for, far worse.

Captain Daniels walked across the lab and flopped down onto the large lounge chair the General had vacated not too long before. The options he had assessed before contacting the General didn't take into account his current situation. Basically, he felt that the decision came down to either getting the best possible analysis, or getting a politically correct, but less useful analysis from somewhere else. Viewing it in another way, his gut told him one thing, but his desire to keep his rank told him another. Weighing in on the gut side, he believed that this was an important investigation to General Cochise; so important in fact that she was personally doing a lot of the work. He doubted she had ever been actively involved in a murder investigation before this one. She was more than involved, really. She, an old line Apache, was going around and digging up pieces of a human skeleton with her bare hands. He was not old line Apache or even Comanche, but he knew of the intense Apache fear of the dead and the horrors of ghost sickness. He in fact recalled the General expressing her concern

for Captain Atwell who had found the first set of
bone squares in the burial ground. She had said
she was considering Atwell for a psychiatric
evaluation because he had been digging and
collecting things from grave dirt. Now the same
Captain Atwell was traveling with the General to
investigate a third body, and they again would
probably be digging for human remains. Appraising
the investigation in these serious and morbid
terms, he knew he had to take a risk and get the
squares genetically analyzed by the best lab he
could find. He had to do this even if he became a
scapegoat for some future political fallout. He
would go to the Comanche Nation with the pieces of
bone. He was basically a natural bridge between
the two Nations anyway, having crossed over from
one to the other. As such, he had a better chance
than most Apache of venturing down this thorny path
unscathed. After all, he had bloodlines in the
Comanche Nation, and he should try to keep in
contact with them even though most of them had
given him up as a lost cause when he crossed over.

     He didn't move from the lounger for another
two hours. It would take him longer than that to
build up his resolve again, but it was a good
start.

     The sun was gradually dropping out of the sky
as the captain and the General neared the location
of the third body. Seeing so much green and so
many trees along the way, she had a brief flashback
of her trip into the Cherokee Nation. Being from
the desert, she had never really appreciated trees.
And now staring into the gloomy darkness that had
already taken over the forest, she still didn't.
No matter how many times she had to venture into
it, the forest was unnatural to her and put her on
edge. None of that was helped by their continuing
Jaagé rocket trip into the heart of the Shawnee
Nation. She was buzzing with adrenaline, and they
hadn't even started their search. At nightfall, in
the middle of nowhere and at the edge of a farm
field, they would probably have the place to
themselves. The body would of course be gone by
the time they arrived now, but the crime scene

should still be marked. If not, and not knowing
the investigative thoroughness of the Shawnee
police, she had gotten the GPS coordinates of the
scene from one of the Apache satellites through the
news feed before they even left the Apache Military
Complex in El Paso. She had already decided that
they would camp at the site if necessary to do a
proper search. The Jaagé had been loaded up for
them while they had still been in the air, and they
would even have tools to work with on this go
around. Now thinking about the digging, she tried
to push the thought that they were searching for
human remains as far out of her mind as she could.
Had she dwelled on it too much near Knoxville, she
would never have found the squares. Of course,
once she had found the first one, the excitement of
the find had carried her through the rest of the
dig. But that was why she had brought Atwell with
her now. He could do the actual grubbing in the
dirt for the bone pieces, and she would set him up
for that psych eval when they got back to
civilization.

Atwell had slowed the Jaagé down tremendously
in the growing darkness as he tried to find roads
that would take them where they needed to go. They
could have practically driven directly to the
coordinates if they were in the desert, but in the
Shawnee Forest, the damn trees stood firmly in
their way. What had that farmer been planting out
there in the middle of the forest anyway? She
doubted if it could be legal when it was hidden
away in all of the stupid trees.

The Nations had suffered the consequences from
their share of illegally grown crops throughout the
years. In the early days, the Shawnee Forest had
been a major hotbed of illegal activity. Hidden
among the trees, the crops had been almost
invisible to the investigative methods at the time.
Even when the crops could be found, the area was
difficult to access by anyone unfamiliar with the
area. As technology improved, this all changed.
Unfortunately, so did the sophistication of the
people growing the illegal crops.

With the rapid evolution of molecular
genetics, the world had changed dramatically in a

short period of time. Simple and legal things were genetically altered to the point that they could no longer be viewed as benign. The more complex they became, the worse it all got.

Marijuana had once been not only legal, but also prevalent in the Americas. As a medicinal herb, the people of the Nations had used it for centuries. But the high potency, genetically altered marijuana that was developed over the years had eventually been made illegal. This happened following a rash of teenage overdoses on the stuff due to the fact that it became so powerful that it could be extremely unpredictable and at its worst even deadly. But the genetic alterations continued beyond there, initially in all probability to evade detection and produce the same product. Unfortunately, like most good things gone bad it didn't stop there and the genetic alterations ultimately created plants that naturally, if you could call it that produced a virtual cocktail of hallucinogens, amphetamines and opiate-like derivatives that could put down an elephant. The harsh reality was that first time users overdid it about seventy-five percent of the time, and the number of resultant deaths had been unimaginable prior to the development of these altered plants.

The most disturbing thing to the general was that the plants had eventually been developed to blend in perfectly with the hemp crops grown throughout the Nations for other than illicit purposes. With the further aid of modern technology, the plants had somehow seemingly been everywhere at once. The hemp industry had been decimated by the plants, or more specifically, by the massive number of deaths attributed to them. The Council had invested millions already into research to explicitly identify the cocktail hemp, but it remained a major problem. The Nations of the Council still relied heavily on hemp as a renewable resource, and there were few reasonably viable alternatives.

With a sudden lurch, the Jaagé came to a stop in the middle of an open, unplanted field. She had lost track of their progress while her thoughts were swallowed up in Council matters. By GPS, they were barely off the appropriate coordinates, and as she had hoped, there wasn't a trace of human presence anywhere to be seen. That included crime scene tape, again to her disgust. But then who would put up crime scene tape in a plowed farm field?

After they got out and stretched their legs for a while, she monitored her GPS watch as she plodded through the field that was already well lit with starlight and Luna at three quarters. The coordinates from the news feed quickly came up, but they could have easily found the spot by the tire-flattened earth that marked a large section of the field. The captain clicked on a large flashlight, and the area around them lit up brighter than day. Neither one of them having spoken a word in several hours, the captain's voice startled the General when he spoke the obvious.

"This is it General Cochise."

Looking at him with an expression indicating he might as well have said two plus two was four, she tried to rein in her irritation. He was a good officer and she couldn't afford to shoot him quite yet. He would be the one meticulously digging for pieces of bone pretty soon, and beyond that he didn't seem to be particularly dimwitted.

"Do you think?" She asked, now trying to hold in a chuckle. The road trip to that point was clearly wearing on both of them.

"Sir…oh, I'm sorry, Sir." He stammered, his face quickly turning red even in the harsh and brilliant artificial light.

"It's O.K. captain." She said calmly. "You'll get to work off your road trance when you start looking for bone squares."

Rank had its privileges, but she didn't usually consider smart-ass remarks directed at her soldiers as one of them. She hadn't achieved her rank by demeaning her fellow officers, no matter how far down the command chain they were and it wouldn't help her now.

Walking more easily across the well-compacted dirt, she quickly made it to the very edge of the field, and what she imagined was the spot where the body had been. It was also heavily trampled, but

by boot prints, not tires. In fact, the trampled
area pretty clearly outlined what had once been the
body, and there wasn't a trace of anything from the
body still there superficially. The crime scene
crew had done a thorough job in that regard.
Fortunately, what the general was really looking
for should be in the soil that remained mostly
undisturbed at her feet. She had little doubt that
there would be a number of human bone squares
there. Just how many was becoming a better
question for her now.

"I'll go pull the Jaagé up to here." She said
without thinking twice about it, and started
walking back toward the vehicle.

The captain, a horrified look on his face, ran
past her and said as he passed. "I'll get it, Sir."

He apparently felt he had somehow missed a
cue, and wasn't going to make another stupid
mistake. Surprised by his response, she kept
walking to the Jaagé and climbed in shortly after
he did.

"I'm fully capable of driving the Jaagé,
captain." She said as she turned to face him.

With the unchanged look of horror on his face,
the captain stammered "Yes, Sir. I know, Sir."

Quickly understanding the situation with the
captain, she pointed to where she wanted to go, and
tried to pick the words to tell the captain that
she was heavily involved in this investigation, and
she would be actively participating in all aspects
of it, including the dig. But unable to think of
anything before they stopped at the dig site, she
decided to forget it, and climbed back out of the
Jaagé without a word. He would figure it out on
his own.

Opening the rear of the Jaagé, she started
pulling tools out and walking them the short
distance to the dig. The captain joined in after a
few moments hesitation, and they finished moving
the tools in silence. With the Jaagé still running
and the headlights on, the dig was even more
brilliantly lit. They would have no trouble
working at night with so much light. After making
a grid over the site with stakes and string, they
both began the tedious work of removing and

straining the soil. Freshly plowed, the job was
easier than it had even been in the Cherokee
Nation's rich loamy soil, but still tiresome after
a long day. Gradually, they made their way through
the quadrants. As layer after layer in each
quadrant of the grid yielded nothing, the small
amount of drive left in the General sputtered out.
They were getting deep enough that the bottom of
the dig was now lost in shadows, so the captain got
a high-powered lantern out of the Jaagé, hung it
over the hole, and they kept digging. When they
were down more than a foot across the entire grid,
they sullenly stopped. The squares the captain had
found at the burial ground had been barely below
the surface, maybe half an inch at most. The
squares she had found in the Cherokee Nation had
been a little deeper, but still probably no more
than two inches deep. They had already gone down
more than six times that depth, and their square
count stood at zero.

"Damn!" The General exclaimed after staring at
the hole for a couple of minutes. "We should have
looked at the body before we came out here."

Too tired to think, the captain simply
responded "Sir?"

"The body, captain. I didn't look at the
body. I saw the first two bodies in person and had
absolute confirmation that they had been scalped.
I had become so sure of what we would find out here
that I skipped a vital step in the investigations
that I had done on the other victims."

The captain put the pieces together, and
slowly said "And this body wasn't scalped?"

"I think it was, but we won't know for sure
until we see it, or at least have the autopsy
report. I knew better than to trust the media
report. I knew better and we came immediately out
here anyway. But even without the scalping,
there's another major problem, no squares, and I'd
say without them this body doesn't fit the
pattern."

Frustrated and exhausted, the General pulled a
bed role out of the Jaagé, spread it on the ground,
and collapsed. She was out before she had a chance
to start thinking. The captain, tired as he was,

propped himself against the side of the Jaagé and solemnly stood watch. They should have brought more people he thought as he struggled to stay awake. They needed a full team like they had gotten in the desert. If the General decided to expand the dig, they would be in way over their heads. Looking slowly around at the vast stretch of freshly plowed field visible in the moonlight, the situation looked pretty hopeless from his perspective. The little squares in the desert had been so easy to find, he had anticipated the same here. Well, not really, he hadn't put any thought into it before now. It was a good thing he hadn't. He was already stretching the General's patience and it would have been worse if he had a bad attitude. With this thought in mind and after what seemed an eternity, he looked at his watch to see that twelve minutes had passed. He wouldn't last long like this. Deciding activity would keep him awake, he turned the Jaagé headlights off and killed the engine. No need to light up the dig or the woods or the field beyond the woods he thought, a faint smile creeping to his face. It wasn't even funny. Serious trouble… he was in serious trouble.

Now he needed something else to do to stay awake. He would fall asleep standing up if he stayed in one place too long. Couldn't have that, the General was already starting to think he was a moron. He would have to walk a perimeter. There was nothing else he could do if he wanted to stay awake.

After two hours of mindlessly dragging his feet through the dirt and more laps than he wanted to think about, the General abruptly sat up and scared the crap out of him. With a little adrenaline boost, he felt more alert than he really cared to be. The General's voice brought another burst of adrenaline into his system.

"Captain, what the hell are you doing?"

Still on autopilot, the captain responded, "Keeping watch, Sir."

"Damnit captain, you're supposed to be sleeping!" She exclaimed.

"Sit down, captain. And that's an order."

With what appeared to be a large effort, the

captain broke his robotic stride and turned to walk back to the Jaagé. He had practically been sleep walking, he imagined before his mind went blank again. Pulling out another bedroll, he collapsed to the ground a few feet from the General. They were both asleep as soon as their heads hit the ground.

The quiet windless night was disturbed an hour later by the crackle of old fallen leaves in the woods. The crackles multiplied intermittently and then began to tail off. Hesitantly, the pack of dogs skirted the soldier's camp in the soft quiet earth, working their way to the center of the makeshift camp with deliberate intent. The body they had returned for was gone, and the smell of death only faintly lingered. But there were other bodies here now, and the animals continued to work their way in with the expectation of more meat to come. This patch of woods had fed them several times over the past months and it looked like it would keep providing for them. What they found there they found in no other place. What they found there had changed them. They would never again be man's best friends.

CHAPTER 9

Dead asleep on the ground by the Apache military Jaagé, the captain and general were seemingly oblivious to their surroundings. They had barely been asleep, but camped in the open field, their military tuned brains were still aware. It was survival instinct magnified beyond that of a normal human's. The dogs slowly circling them in the soft dirt were nearly soundless, but their stealth was betrayed by a remnant of the smallest dog's past life with humans. The rabies tag still attached to its collar clinked twice as the dog stumbled over a small mound of dirt. The sound was soft, but it brought both of the soldiers to their feet before the dogs could make it back into the woods. Suddenly awake and tense as hell, the captain bolted after the dogs without thinking and was halfway through the woods before he tripped over a pile of sticks and came crashing back to the ground. Damn, he thought as he watched the dogs clear the woods and dart up over a hill into another field.

The General didn't move during the captain's wild escapade. Hearing him crash to the forest floor, she grabbed the lantern and walked to the edge of the woods where she called out, "Captain, are you all right?" Following a brief burst of rustling dead leaves, she could see the captain stand up, and then crouch back down to the ground.

"General, you had better come here, Sir." He yelled back. She could see him stand back up, but he didn't move away from the place he had fallen down. What now, she thought to herself as she carried the lantern into the woods heading towards the captain. As the light of her lantern gradually lit the captain and his surroundings, she noticed that the captain's left boot was buried above the ankle in sticks and dead leaves. She couldn't recognize the elongated mound his foot was protruding from until she was standing beside him and nearly on top of it herself. The leaf-covered rib cage was human, she was pretty sure, and it had taken a hold of the captain's boot like a bear trap. To the General, this suggested that the remains were fresh enough for the ribs to spring aside as the captain's foot came down on them. The bones also seemed to be the flexible and resilient ones of a younger person, having not been crushed or at least snapped by the captain's weight on impact. Quickly scanning the area, she didn't immediately identify any other bones protruding through the leaf litter. But it was too dark, and the lantern seemed to make her quick search worse by casting shadows from every single vertical piece of debris on the ground. They would have to do a careful search in full daylight, and they would need a full team.

"Captain, can you get yourself out of there?" The General asked, knowing she wouldn't be able to summon the nerve to handle the rotting chunk of ribcage now or even next year.

"I believe so, Sir." He said as he used his

other foot for leverage against the ribs, and easily extricated his boot from the remains. The ribs, still supported by a significant amount of connective tissue, popped back into place like they were spring loaded. Not appearing shaken at all, the captain looked at the general and calmly said, "Seems to be kind of fresh, Sir."

The situation finally registered somewhere deep among the General's Apache beliefs. With a shudder, she took a reflexive step back from the captain and the corpse. She abruptly also felt a sense of amazement that the captain hadn't been disturbed by his foot being buried in a recently dead human's ribcage.

"Doesn't this bother you, captain?" She asked, having difficulty even thinking about the situation.

Multigenerational Apache himself, the captain immediately knew what the general was alluding to. Stepping back from the remains, he turned to directly face her, and therefore also avoid looking at the body any longer.

"I'm trying very hard not to think about it, Sir. Very hard."

Somewhat relieved, she turned rapidly and headed back towards the Jaagé. Muttering to herself just loud enough for the captain to hear, she said, "I'll accept that for now, captain."

By mid-morning, and after General Cochise had basically greased a boatload of Shawnee Nation palms, the area swarmed with her own Apache Nation military personnel and Shawnee Nation law enforcement officers. She wasn't overjoyed about the law enforcement presence, but she understood it, and did her best to have her people work with them. The scene was huge after all, and they needed every pair of eyes they could get to search it. The dogs and other scavengers had been busy, and the members of her own team were now finding remains scattered half a mile out into the surrounding fields and forest.

Unfortunately, the local law enforcement involvement also carried with it a significant media presence. This the General could have definitely done without, she thought as she looked out one of the command center's darkened windows. Along with a sizable NNS crew, a dozen Shawnee Nation news stations now had small makeshift camps surrounding her large and very imposing mobile command center. The magnitude of the current search had most likely leaked out through one of the local police stations for a few bucks, but rationally she knew they couldn't have contained it anyway. The news crews probably hadn't even left the area after reporting the day before since the autopsy results were still pending and it was such a horrendous find. With that thought, she asked a communications tech to connect her to the morgue where the corpse found the day before had been taken. The locals should have the autopsy results, or at least be able to answer her questions by now. If there were tool marks on the skull, she could settle in there in the field for a few days and see the new search results first hand.

When the Apache com tech didn't get an answer at the morgue after several tries, she decided to take a better look at the site map the team was developing as they came across more of the scattered remains. The General turned to the large communications monitor occupying a wall of the command center. The monitor was built into one of the many pop-outs that literally doubled the already large interior of the Mobile Command Center's cargo trailer shell. As detailed as the map was, it filled the screen and was difficult to take in when she stood too close to it. A chair on the opposite wall of the pop-out provided her with a better 'big picture' view of what they were dealing with, and she could still clearly see each and every glowing red dot that was indicating a find. Staring for a few minutes at the screen, she found the increasing number of dots disturbing since they had a long way to go on the preliminary search. If they were in the heart of some hunters' favorite butcher grounds, most of what they were finding wouldn't be human and it would seriously screw up the search. She didn't believe that was the case, but she knew that it was better to be safe than sorry. With that disturbing thought, she felt a sudden need to see exactly what was being logged in as human remains by her team. A few seconds later, she stepped off of the last of the Command Center's retractable steps onto the soft field, and walked towards the nearest actively searching team member she could see. The General didn't know the soldier, but it didn't matter. Her rank bands indicated she was a lieutenant in the Apache military and it was pretty easy to build a question around that information even when she was as tired as she felt right then.

"Lieutenant, what have you found so far?" She asked sharply.

Just finishing the transmission of the GPS coordinates of her last find, the lieutenant snapped to attention. She was at the edge of the woods a good 20 yards west of where the dog-mauled body had been found.

"Long bone, Sir, femur if it's human." She said vacantly, staring out into the field.

The scatter of bones at the lieutenant's feet practically screaming "POOR INVESTIGATION" by the locals in her mind, the General said "At ease," and tried to mentally connect the bleached and disconnected bones before she would feel the urge to step back from them. They looked human, and they also looked a hell of a lot older than the original body or the rib cage. Pushing the limits of her comfort, she continued her assessment, and counted five other bones close to the one just recorded, then took her big step back. Unlike herself and Atwell, members of other tribes and recent transfers to the Apache Nation predominantly made up the search teams. None of the team members had the slightest difficulty in dealing with the dead or human remains of any kind, and each and every one of them might as well have been aliens from another planet as far as the General was concerned. They were not and never would be truly Apache in their beliefs, and in the current situation, it was a damn good thing.

"Keep it up, lieutenant", the general said as she brushed past her, and made her way to the next closest member of her team. A few more spot checks like that and she would feel a little better about

the search. Of course, she would feel a hell of a
lot better if they found a skull with clearly
recognizable tool marks out there. After getting
no answer at the morgue, she was beginning to think
that it might be weeks before a medical examiner in
the middle of nowhere would come up with the
autopsy results, and she was way too impatient for
that kind of crap.

The next team member in her path had what
appeared to be a spread of human ribs, also
completely stripped of flesh and heavily weathered.
The ribs could have belonged to the femur she had
just seen based on the similarity in their
appearance. That would make for a minimum of three
bodies at the site up to that point, since the rib
cages of both the original and Atwood's bodies were
intact. The number was already climbing and it
wasn't a good picture, not a good picture at all.

The squawk of the General's belt radio
instantly caught her attention, and she pushed the
talk button to say, "Go ahead."

The captain had the only other radio out there
tuned to her current frequency, and his slightly
distorted and crackly voice chirped out of the
speaker molded into her belt. If she were using a
headset linked to the radio, they could have talked
privately. But she hated headsets, and there was
clearly nothing private about their investigation
at that point.

"General Cochise, one of the team members has
found something I think you need to see."

Pushing the talk button, she said, "Be right
there, captain," and started off in his direction.
He had been searching near a drainage ditch on the
other side of the patch of woods, and she believed
she could partially see him through the tree
trunks. As she passed the ribcage Atwood had
buried his boot in the day before, she saw that the
area around it had been pretty thoroughly cleared
of leaves, and she now easily saw other bones
strewn about that had been impossible to see
before. Her quick appraisal was that they were
probably associated with the now fully visible
ribcage based again solely on there mutual level of
decay. After scanning the area a second time, she

realized that there wasn't a skull there even
though the corpse had spent far less time in the
woods than the previous one had. One skull would
help determine if these bodies were the work of the
sergeant's killer, or some other nut job butcher.
That extremely disturbing thought brought her back
to her foolish belief that serial killers were a
rarity in the lands of the Nations of the
Intertribal Council. Seasoned soldier or not, she
seemed to be capable of creating whitewashed
fantasies on a pretty grand scale. It had to be
the stress she put herself under, she thought.
Maybe she was the one needing the psych eval.

The General broke free of the woods about
fifteen feet from the captain, and didn't
immediately see what he had called her over for.
He stood on the far edge of a wide and deep ditch
as he stared down into the weeds surrounding three
actively searching Apache soldiers.

"What is it, captain?" She said as she walked
up to the edge of the ditch directly across from
him. He pointed down into the ditch without saying
a word. A little irritated, the General looked
down into the ditch towards the three soldiers, and
her heart leapt in her chest. At her soldiers'
feet lay four human skulls, some still partially
covered with decomposing flesh. Without having to
get any closer, she saw that two had clearly been
scalped, the bone showing prominently like islands
on top of the otherwise hair covered skulls. The
other two were already bare bone and weathered like
the femur and ribs she had just seen. Looking back
up at the captain, she couldn't help but smile. He
had been right in his earlier remark. This was
definitely it. They now had a focal point of
probable linked murders in an inhabited but
sparsely populated section of the Nations. People
who went missing around there were likely to be
missed. If they could ID the skulls, they might
find a commonality, and that could take them back
to the killer.

"Good work." She said, receiving a return of
quickly fading smiles in response to her own. The
General's smile then dissolved with those of the
soldiers as the grim nature of their find swallowed

her back up and left her a little sick to her
stomach. She had seen many things in combat,
things that would turn the average person's stomach
in the blink of an eye. But this was different.
The killer was deliberately striking at the core of
her native beliefs, her beliefs and millions of
others. Whoever was doing the killing was a
monster akin to the ones in their ancient
mythology. Not literally, of course, but just as
frightening as the stories she had heard as a
child. Just like any other story, there had been
a beginning to this and she was determined to write
the end.

Turning back, she deliberately retraced her
steps to the rib cage the captain had buried his
foot in. As soon as the forensics unit did their
work and cleared the remains, she had another
project to take care of, or at least to supervise.
With the scatter of the bleached bones, they were
unlikely to find a clearly evident excavation site.
But the rib cage may have been left in place by the
scavengers. At least she hoped it had. She still
wanted the additional link of the square bone
fragments set below one of the bodies there to
guide her in some obscure but familiar direction.
It would have been easier to let that part of her
investigation slide. Without the satellite images
at the burial ground, they would never have seen
the killer sweeping the ground with his hands, and
therefore, would never have found the squares. But
they would still be hunting the killer, and
probably nothing else to that point would have
changed. Maybe in some bizarro alternate universe
that's the way it had happened. She could also be
living in a wasteland area death camp with her
people having been overrun by invaders and left
struggling to survive. But that could never
happen, and the squares were part of her
investigation, a significant part still from her
perspective even though she didn't know why yet.
Native death camps, where had that crazy thought
come from?

Refocusing, the General decided to get another
good look at the site map. They would still need
to excavate any area with a significant

concentration of remains. The data had been coming in quickly, and some reasonable dig sites might have already become clear or could be approaching that point. She would pull in more teams if necessary and they would excavate the whole damn map area if that's what it took.

As she climbed back into the mobile command center, she realized that the makeshift media camp had grown by several vehicles. In particular, the insignias of the Pima and Comanche Nations stood out and pushed her a little further into her morose thoughts. The word was definitely out and it had been unavoidable, but she felt like they were being spied on all the same.

Two com techs addressed the General as soon as she opened the command center door, seemingly competing for her attention. Apparently unable to ascertain which one of them had the most important information to give her, both techs rattled on and she couldn't make out a damn thing either one was saying. Directing her full attention toward the tech who had been trying to contact the local morgue, the other tech backed quickly down and she could finally understand one of them. The tech had gotten through, but the autopsy results wouldn't be available for at least another six hours because it would be nearly that long before the pathologist even got to the morgue. She briefly entertained the idea of flying in Dr. Desoto, the medical examiner from the Cherokee Nation, but quickly let the idea go when she began to estimate the amount of political crap she would have to wade through to avoid stepping on the local guy's toes. It would have been simple if she hadn't been on the Council because she would have flown him in without a second thought and let the politicians negotiate the details after the fact no matter how ugly it got. Those days were gone for her. The military commander and the Apache in her both missed them.

Turning to the second tech, her heart went into overdrive as she recognized the man's face that had replaced the wall sized site map on the main monitor.

"Council member Parker," slipped out of her mouth before she could contain her surprise. His

strong, dark features had always reminded her
vaguely of her husband and it had been
disconcerting under normal Council circumstances.
Her surprise shifted to concern and then rapidly to
suspicion before he could even get his first word
out.

"Council member….General.., I'm sorry, how
should I address you under these circumstances?" he
managed to say with a look that, practiced or not,
screamed sincerity. Like Rand, he was very good at
what he did, and she couldn't allow herself to
forget it.

Now oozing hard earned composure, the General
looked directly into the monitor's camera and
responded, "Either will do."

"Very well then, General and Council member
Cochise, thank you for taking my call." He said
without further hesitation.

Thinking she hadn't really had a choice in the
matter and also thinking that the damn com tech
needed a formal reprimand, she narrowed her usually
large blue eyes and paused briefly. The call was
unusual between Council members and virtually
impossible for her to interpret considering the
history of Apache—Comanche relations. The level of
her suspicion multiplied immeasurably, but Parker
calmly went on.

"I know this is unusual and I apologize for
disturbing you. But I have just received word from
one of my labs that your Nation and you in
particular have important samples of some kind that
you need to have urgently analyzed."

Again taken by surprise, "What?" slipped out
before she could rein in her mouth.

Seeing his advantage, but casually and
deliberately disregarding it, Parker smoothly went
on. His experiences with military people had
taught him to be clear and straight to the point
when dealing with them. They were generally
intolerant of chitchat, and he suspected General
Cochise was no different. Even so, he hadn't
expected her response, and he needed to approach
this more carefully to prevent her from shutting
him out. This was a golden opportunity to begin
the process of mending the long history of poor

Comanche-Apache relations. He believed he had one
shot to do it right or wait possibly years for
another window. He was patient, but not that
patient.

"A scientist in one of my Nation's…well
actually my own personal lab, had direct contact
with the Apache military complex in El Paso earlier
today. In particular, Captain Daniels of your
Nation just completed a transmission to my facility
requesting urgent, yet detailed and discreet
genetic analysis of a collection of small bone
fragments of, as he described them, great
importance to you."

Standing stiffly in front of her wall monitor
with her arms crossed, she tried to mentally race
through a list of implications of Parker's very
unexpected call. But first and foremost thought
was that Daniels had lost his damn mind! What was
he possibly thinking given thinking was involved at
all! Parker and his lab weren't going to assist
them now or even in the next hundred million years.
Their Nations were staunch political enemies and
would undoubtedly be to the end of time. As little
as she understood it, she had quickly learned to
accept it after joining the Council. Before that,
the whole Apache-Comanche issue had been
irrelevant. Painfully recalling her previous
indifference, she prepared herself for a berating
onslaught from Parker. It had to be the only
reason he would contact her directly. Her other
considerations would have to wait. She needed to
shift gears and portray the Council member aspect
of her life even if it killed her. With extreme
difficulty, she pulled on her smiling politician
mask last used at the impromptu meeting with Rand
only a day before.

"Yes, Council member Parker, Daniels has
indicated to me that your labs are the best of
their kind in the world."

Now seeing a brief and unexpected look of
surprise on Parker's face, she felt lost for a
second and struggled to recalculate what had just
happened. Remarkably, Parker now seemed to be as
uncomfortable as she was. The slight break in his
thick politician's veneer was monumental. She knew

he could sling the bullshit with the best of them and she had never seen even the slightest crack in his Council member persona. She was virtually a political amateur and prone to multiple mistakes on a daily basis when in Parker's element, but not him. It was his element, damnit! He was a politician through and through. Even then his response smacked of sincerity and what he said next seemed to confirm it in her mind.

"Why….thank you, General Cochise. I am honored that you trust me, my lab and my Nation in assisting you." A genuine smile took over his entire face. She had learned at least that much about people and politics.

"It's a go then?" She asked, still too disarmed to mutter anything else.

"Yes, absolutely! Excellent! I will make your specimens my lab's top priority. Your Captain Daniels can provide the details of your needs to my lab directly and I will monitor the lab's progress personally and provide results to you as they become available."

"Very good. Thank you Council member Parker. We will give you our full trust in this matter."

Still smiling, Parker cut the link and settled back into his chair. As far as he could tell, it seemed to have gone O.K. He felt a little exhilarated and wished he had someone to celebrate with. His plans were moving forward more quickly than he had expected, and if nothing else, he had earned some time away from Pueblo Bonito and the Council.

At the other end of the link, the General took a seat in the first chair she could find. The last few minutes had been surreal, and she needed time to process them. She recalled giving Daniels control of the bone chip analysis, but she had never expected this when she did. Even though Daniels had moved directly from the Comanche Nation to a position in the Apache military, he couldn't have the pull to accomplish something like this. She would never have given him credit for the guts to even try, and yet here she sat having just spoken to the extremely pleasant and cooperative Council representative of the Comanche Nation, the

Apache Nation's greatest enemy in the Intertribal Council.

The return of their rapidly progressing site map to the wall monitor slowly pulled the General out of her thoughts. If the killer had left his calling card there, they would find it and Parker would have more bone fragments to analyze. The Comanche representative Parker of all people, he was actually the most unbelievable aspect of their whole investigation now. Staring somewhat vacantly at the monitor, she realized the data dots on the map had accumulated fairly significantly in the short time she had been outside. She decided it was time to call and get more people out to the site. By the time they made it out from their units in the surrounding Nations, several bone cluster areas would be fully processed and logged. The carefully planned excavations could then proceed immediately.

The General's thoughts shifted again, and she recalled the large gray clouds slowly coming towards them from the west. Spring in the Shawnee Nation could serve up some pretty wild weather and she wouldn't be surprised if they were hit with a downpour before they finished. Thinking of the two excavations she had already done, she developed a greater sense of urgency that pulled her fully out of her daze. She could clearly imagine the shallow digs they were about to make filling with water. That would be bad enough, but spring weather also brought lightning and twisters to the Shawnee Nation, both of which she could live without on most days, well, every day. She needed to keep busy and squash the worry out of her mind. They couldn't control the weather yet but they could prepare for it, or better yet avoid it. They would try to do both. If she were an optimist, she wouldn't have been so worried. But she had shed most of her optimism with the death of her husband, so they would prepare for the worst.

CHAPTER 10

The wind roared through the General's camp
threatening to dismantle everything her soldiers
had erected to protect the site from the rain. No
downpour yet, but it was coming. She could feel
heaviness in the air a thousand times more
oppressive than what she was used to in the desert.
She couldn't live here, and She really couldn't
imagine who could. Bad weather was for people who
didn't know any better, or didn't have a choice,
She thought as she looked up to the sky to see
black clouds swallowing the previous brightness.
Damn! Crew five had better get their asses in gear
and protect their dig, she thought. The other
seven crews were already starting to excavate
inside their wind-stressed canvas shells. Sandbags
rested above the ones on a slope and the hope was
the whole area wouldn't flood. They would use
pump trucks if they had to, but the trucks hadn't
made it out to the site yet. As noted before, the
General prepared for the worst. If she could have
extracted the entire area and moved it to El Paso,
she would have. But there wasn't enough time for
that. There never was enough time for anything.

"General." Captain Atwell blurted out as he
came rushing around the corner of the command
center. She had assigned him to the site in the
woods where he had found the ribcage. She figured
since he had inadvertently found it, he should have
the satisfaction of discovering the bone chips if
they were there. He was leading and supervising
team one, but she suspected he was actively digging
along with everyone else. Of course the dirt on
his knees was a pretty big clue.

"We've hit bone chips already." He continued
as he approached her. Of all the people out there,
he was the only one with prior specific knowledge
of the fragments, aside from the General. She had
no doubt now. The killer had been there and she
had proof of it even if the rest of the crews
struck out. Her heart sped up a little as the
captain abruptly turned back around and she
followed him back to his site. As they pulled the
tent flap back, the brightness of the well-lit
interior was a dramatic contrast to the near dark

woods around it. Black clouds continued to fill the sky. The rain couldn't be far off.

Looking down, the General observed an extremely shallow excavation of maybe a half an inch in depth. The chips were protruding out of the soil on end, and her thoughts flashed back to the Cherokee Nation fragments she had found.

"Is this the way the fragments were buried in the desert?" She asked as the question popped into her head.

"Yes, Sir." The captain responded as he stooped down to take a closer look at the dig. Two successive camera flashes blinded her for a few seconds, but when her vision returned, she repeated her count.

"Only eleven?" She asked, wondering if some of the squares had already been removed.

"This is it so far, Sir." Atwood replied, looking quickly around at the other three team members. They all nodded and continued their work.

"What do you mean, so far?" She asked as her brain forced her to recount the fragments for a fifth time. There were still only eleven.

We're going to go deeper to see if there are any more on another level, Sir" He reported matter-of factly.

"There won't be." She mumbled to herself, feeling pretty confident in the thought. "Were they in multiple layers in our Nation, captain?" She asked, having a quick rush of adrenaline as she questioned whether she had missed any squares herself in the Cherokee Nation.

"No, Sir, but we're going to be thorough all the same."

The General looked into his eyes and nodded. She had taken the single layer for granted at her own dig and then assumed it had been the same in the Apache Nation. For whatever reason, relief flooded in and she thought back to the previous fragment counts. They now had finds of eleven, seventeen, and eighteen. The counts had to be significant and the only reasonable conclusion that occurred to her was that they represented the number of kills. If that were the case, fifteen more scalped and bludgeoned bodies were yet to be found. Ten preceded the current one and five occurred after it. The decay of the bodies was consistent with this and suggested that some of the other remains out there had been left even before number eleven. The body currently at the morgue would be at least number nineteen. Nineteen, she thought…for such a small number, it was too damn big as a body count. They needed to find the monster responsible and put an end to his activities at all costs.

"Captain," She said, "Come with me."

Pushing through the tent flap, the smell of rain hit the General's nose and she knew their prep time was up, and that meant crew five's prep time was also up. Her initial thought to check on all of the other crews on her way back to the command center would have to wait. Five was under the gun. The captain and the General took off at a slow trot in the direction of crew five and quickly found them prepared and inside. They were just starting to dig and it seemed logical to wait them out and keep dry. The only problem was her impatience. Before she knew it, she had joined the dig and Atwell had followed suit. As the rain pounded the tent, the six of them made quick work of the excavation and were down five inches before too long. There were no fragments unfortunately. They went a little deeper just to be safe, but nothing changed. Site five was a dead end, but there were still at least six more possibilities out there based on the bone distribution.

They moved on to the next closest tent and found that the crew had uncovered four fragments and had gone down a foot deeper afterwards for good measure. The chip counts were now four, eleven, seventeen, and eighteen and the pattern remained consistent with her current theories. A little while later, she heard less rain pounding on the canvas, looked out and decided to go back to the command center. Atwood followed her, but stopped at the next site to assist with their dig. The General had gotten pretty cold from the heavy rain that had soaked her already and she needed a cup of coffee both to warm her up and to boost her energy. By the time she made it to the command center, she was wringing wet and starting to shiver from the cold rain. As much prep as they had done, Atwood had taken her off guard when he came to tell her about the first find and she hadn't been personally prepared for the rain. She felt the findings to that point were worth it. She also wanted to look at the remains logs corresponding to the dead end site. The overall bone pattern at that site had looked as promising as the others, but maybe it was a quality and not a quantity issue. After all, they had found four skulls in a single pile in the ditch. Other factors could have contributed to the dig site as well and could contribute to any other dead ends they hit.

"Any word from the morgue?" She asked the com tech as she sloshed up into the command center.

"No, Sir. But their estimated time is nearly up."

Nodding, she worked her way past several other soldiers and made it back to the bunkroom to get a dry uniform. Fortunately, there was already a fresh pot of coffee brewing and she soon felt both warm and dry. She decided it was easy to forget how significant these little things in life could be.

Back in front of the massive site map display, she got a printout of the log for the empty dig area and couldn't see any reason for the lack of findings. It didn't really matter. With what they already had, the investigation had gotten a major boost. The number of remains they had found there seemed to indicate a fairly long period of activity by the killer in the Shawnee Nation. With number four found there, Shawnee could be his home Nation. They could really use some good information about missing persons in the area now and maybe match skulls with dental records. The Shawnee Nation Investigative Unit would have what they needed. It was time to reinvolve the locals.

Captain Daniels sent the bone squares to the lab his brother and sister worked at in the Comanche Nation as soon as he got their quick response. General Cochise had threatened a psych eval until he told her whom he had contacted. Only

child or not, she had kids, so she understood. For
whatever reason, his own siblings had broken out of
their cold, hard shells and responded like family
instead of using the nasty National enemies
response they usually reserved for Nation traitors.
The General hadn't elaborated, but she seemed to
have a good idea of what was going on. In fact,
she had more sets of squares to be analyzed already
and wanted them done with the others. She also
requested that he be at the lab himself to monitor
progress and directly report to her. He was in
route to the Comanche Nation already and would meet
the new samples at Parker's lab. Again, for
whatever reason, this was all above board and
accepted by Parker and the Comanche Nation. He had
grown up in an environment that was constantly
hostile toward the Apache Nation and now he was
heading back under very different circumstances.
Maybe it was a trap… The idea was more reasonable
than the current reality. He would soon find out.

    His successful talk with General Cochise
having gone even better than his best expectations,
Parker had immediately left Pueblo Bonito for his
home Nation. It was his lab, and he believed his
people were the best in their field, but he had a
deeper interest in the results of their new
project. It had been awhile since he had been in
the lab, and it might feel good for a change.
Though he rarely used it and didn't even
acknowledge it most of the time, he had a doctorate
in molecular biology. But the whole doctor thing
put the politicians off usually, so he had let it
drift away like so many other parts of his pre-
Council life. The knowledge and abilities were
still there, and he would put them to good use for
Council business for the first time in his career.
    The door to his lab swung quietly open as he
approached it. Too much money led to some pretty
wasteful things some of the time he thought as he
passed through. The Council buildings didn't even
have automatic doors. For some reason it felt like
a welcome home anyway and he was still glad he had
them installed.
    "George..Ella." He called out as the automatic

doors closed behind him. Brother and sister molecular biologists, he thought. It was funny how some twins were so different and others almost the same. They weren't actually twins in this case, but two-thirds of a set of triplets, basically the same thing. If he didn't know better, he would have thought some genetic engineering was involved. Sam kind of detracted from that thought anyway, but not totally. He was a scientist after all and probably a good one, well, surely a good one. Maybe it was the name that caused him to head off in his greatly unexpected direction. Names had power. Sam Daniels…there was something not quite right about it. Samuel Daniels wasn't any better. Poor guy, he had grown up taking a lot of shit his brother and sister never experienced. Maybe it was why he fled to the Apache Nation. The Comanche Nation had never really let up on him. He was definitely the odd man out and everyone made it pretty clear to him from the day he was born.

"Edward!" Ella squealed as she ran up and gave him a hug. "Welcome back."

"I hope it's alright if I don't squeal." George said as he came up behind Ella. "I gave that up last week and I'm determined to stop for good."

"Smartass." Ella said as she freed herself from Edward and turned to give George a dirty look.

Smiling because he was truly happy, Parker felt even better than when the automatic doors had greeted him. It was good to be home and even better to be here with friends. "I see you've kept everything intact."

"Genetics doesn't call for much explosives these days." George said, shaking his hand.

"Smartass is right." Edward said, turning to Ella. "Some things never change." Laughing he landed a good, solid flat-handed blow to George's stomach, stealing his breath for a second and surprising him even though he knew it was coming. "I still owe you a few." He said, laughing even harder. It was funny for one of them every time, and Ella still couldn't understand it after nearly fifty years of growing up together.

"Sam's coming." Ella blurted out like an

excited child.

His laughter dying down, Edward finally settled down enough to reply. "I know, El."

All of them smiling now including George, they worked their way to the back of the lab and their private quarters. They might as well catch up in comfort, buzzing through each of their minds. They thought alike most of the time to the extent that they used to joke about him being swapped at birth and replaced with Sam. Of course, Sam never found it as funny as they did, and it probably added to his alienation. Kids would be kids and the thought of Sam drifting away didn't seem so terrible now that he was coming to work with them.

"We already received the samples." George stated as they pulled three lounge chairs up around a coffee table in Edward's living room.

"Good. Have you started yet?"

"No. We're waiting for the rest to come. And Sam of course." George responded.

"O.K. Not really much of a delay I guess." Edward said, becoming abruptly serious.

"We thought the same." Ella said, also seriously even though thinking alike was usually an in-joke for them.

"Did you look at them?" Edward asked both of them.

"Yes." They both responded simultaneously.

"And..."

"Thirty-five small pieces of bone and that's it. Well, not in total, there are reportedly more on the way." George said, shifting a little in his chair. "Along with Sam, of course." Ending as he hit a comfortable spot.

"When's he getting here?" Edward said, picking up the thought.

"Any time now. We offered to pick him up, but he said an Apache soldier stationed in our Nation would drive him out."

Before they could continue, they all heard a loud "Hello" coming from the front of the lab.

"That didn't sound like Sam." Ella said as she stood up to see who had called out.

"Not unless he had a sex change. That was a woman." George said, receiving an appreciative smack on the top of his head as Ella passed him.

A minute later, she returned with a plain box that was a lot lighter than its size would generally indicate. The label was clearly visible and said Parker Labs, Comanche Nation in bold print.

"It was an Apache soldier." She said.

"Really." Edward said with a little surprise. "Even though they serve as our military protection now I rarely see them."

"Yes, they're very discreet. It's kind of unnerving." George said looking at the box in Ella's hands. "I'm not used to them yet."

"Things are changing, George." Edward said as Ella handed him the box.

"What are you up to now, Ed?" George said with a nearly straight-faced smile. "World peace."

"Smartass, Smartass, Smartass." Ella grumbled, popping him on the head again before sitting back down.

Nothing else had to be said. There were no secrets between them even though Edward was now on the Council. They had discussed everything he was working on repeatedly and they were his closest advisers. Other politicians had more politicians to advise them, but not him. Only genius level scientists would do. Maybe that was why some of the other Nations had so many problems, idiots leading idiots.

The box now open and sample boxes on the coffee table, they each took one and opened it slowly. What was it with Cochise and her little bone chips? They all looked exactly the same no matter how many she sent.

"Any idea what this is about, Ed?" George asked, looking into his lightly occupied sample box.

"Not really, just that it's important to Council member Cochise. Sam will know."

"This is a pretty damn good bridge, don't you think?" George asked, not needing an answer.

"Couldn't have asked for a better one." He said, now also looking more closely at his box's contents. "Did the first batch come separated like this?"

"Seventeen in one and eighteen in another."
Ella answered. "This one has eleven."

"Four here." Said George, looking up to hear
Edward's count.

"Eight." He said. "We'd better keep them well
separated in the lab. They all look the same
superficially and we don't know the significance of
the separation."

Having closed up boxes with four, eight, and
eleven chips, they all had their second box open
for inspection. The counts were again quick, and
they now had sets of four, five, seven, eight, nine
and eleven bone chips.

"That's it." Ella said, rechecking the
shipping box. "No more boxes and not a sliver of
paper with IDs or instructions."

The mystery of the bone chips building, they
all sat back and stared at each other for a few
minutes. They knew what to do with them, of
course. A genetic analysis of every single piece
was necessary. What they would compare the results
against was another story all together.
Simultaneously, they thought 'Sam will know', but
none of them said it this time because it was
strange talking so openly about him after all these
years. The gap had grown pretty wide, and his call
out of nowhere had been extremely unexpected. The
fact that his call also carried with it not only
the opportunity to work together, but also a
mechanism to bring the Comanche and Apache Nations
out of centuries of hostility, even on an embryonic
level, was beyond bizarre. It had to be fate, that
or the workings of some mostly absentee and
negligent god. Comanche or not, they were all
scientists, diviners of fact, and extreme skeptics
of anything bordering on the supernatural. Hard
evidence of the workings behind this would become
evident sooner or later, not a one of them had a
doubt. Of course, politics had already started to
warp Edward, but the other two still had their
heads on straight. Alone, each could carry the
load if necessary.

"I need some coffee…anyone else?" Edward
eventually said, breaking the silence.

"Sure." Two-thirds of the Daniels triplets

said in unison.

Some things never changed, Parker again thought to himself. Some things never changed.

Connecting with the Shawnee Nation Investigative Unit had been easy. They operated on a pretty standard frequency and responded with a pair of agents a hell of a lot faster than autopsies were done in the area. She should have flown DeSoto in, she thought again. Her gut impulses were usually right on the mark whether she wanted to acknowledge them or not.

Remarkably, they had been authorized to tie into the SNIUs computer system and search the limited recorded dental records available along with associated missing persons registries that were barely more extensive. Rand was clearly a master. She didn't have that much power in her Nation and her own credentials now spanned two very powerful aspects of the Apache world. But then, Rand was an ancient. That had to carry quite a bit of weight.

"General, we have a link to the pathologist, Sir." The com tech said, breaking the General's concentration.

She had already found the data output of missing persons to be completely meaningless without the details of each case. That part of the investigation was going to take awhile.

"Bring the morgue link up." She said, rubbing her eyes and thinking she needed some more coffee.

An extremely poor quality image of a kid barely beyond pimples popped onto the wall monitor.

"General, I'm Dr. Wells. I have your results." The kid said. She was surprised he was old enough to talk, but she said, "Go ahead" anyway. Her age was catching up with her. Extensively trained adults were starting to look like toddlers. She could imagine he wouldn't appreciate her first impressions. Her own kids were younger than him, but she didn't have grandchildren yet so she could still maintain the delusion of youth.

"My findings were kind of off the charts, General. It's unlikely they'll be significant to you."

"Off the charts is what I'm looking for, doctor. You can't even imagine."

In obvious disbelief, the pathologist forged on. "Well I don't know how much detail you need. Where do you want me to start?"

"Start with the unusual findings. We can branch out from there."

He said "O.K.", and then paused for an unexpected length of time. "I had difficulty believing my eyes, and I've seen some pretty disturbing things in my time." Wells said, clearly uncomfortable with what he was about to say.

Looking at the face on the monitor with more understanding than he was currently capable of comprehending, the General waited for him to tell her something that was actually becoming commonplace to her. It didn't even make her sick to her stomach or stir up vengeful rage anymore. Ilya O'Connor's death had changed her life. Even as a general in the most powerful military in the world, she found she had lost some innocence, innocence she had no idea was there. Innocence that was that much more precious because it was probably all she had left.

"The man died from cardiac tamponade….and he was both ravaged by animals and…..this is a preliminary finding. I'm having another pathologist look at it."

"Look at what, Dr. Wells?"

"Look at the skull, General. The man was…scalped.."

He fell silent, and then abruptly felt he had to justify what he had just said.

"Tools marks..there are tool marks on the skull. I compared the damage obviously caused by scavengers to the"

Cutting him off and probably alleviating his discomfort, she said "Thank you, Doctor. I have what I need. Let me know if you can identify the body."

In wide-eyed disbelief, the doctor nodded and the link was terminated.

You have no idea, doctor; you have no idea, she thought as she added another piece of data to her mental list of atrocities. If this was any indication of the things to come, the world was in serious trouble. Wherever the bone fragments were, this was probably number nineteen. Nineteen if she was optimistic, but optimism was beyond the scope of her reality now.

CHAPTER 11

The atmosphere in Parker's lab still bordered on icy several hours after Sam arrived. The reunion was far from heart warming due to some initial hesitation from both sides as a result of his long absence. This was exacerbated by Sam's brisk military attitude, and he seemed to be intent on maintaining decorum. Along with his rigid behavior, he had also been dead set on providing a minimum of specifics to the rest of the people in the lab, and hadn't yet wavered in spite of a barrage of questions. Beyond the actual work, he tried his best to stay away from his brother, sister and Edward if at all possible, scurrying away like a roach in the light and not maintaining eye contact with any of them even when saying the few things he did say. The work went on anyway because they all had factors beyond the familial connection that were driving them, one shared factor really, the General. Sam cleaned and prepped the new bone fragments that had arrived at Parker's lab directly from the Shawnee Nation dig site, and the other three worked smoothly in tandem to get an initial but complete and even triplicate analysis of the samples as efficiently as possible.

In spite of Ella's hopeful expectations before Sam arrived, she eventually gave up on her efforts to pull Sam back in. Along with Edward and George, she decided that if this was the way it was going to be, Sam needed to be on his way back to the Apache Nation as soon as possible. The years away had apparently damaged him beyond any hope of reconciliation with them. He had become just another Apache soldier in the Comanche Nation, present but elusive and extremely unsettling. The other two had hit it right on the nose in that regard.

Even with the bad atmosphere in the lab and in spite of their differences, the four all had the same driven quality to their work. They would push through the entire analysis without sleep if they could manage it, only stopping if fatigue started to take a potential toll on their results. As he continued to meticulously clean the fragments of evidence, Sam realized that with the new arrivals they now had seventy-nine perfect little squares of bone so superficially identical to each other that they could have been laser cut on an assembly line, and he was starting to be amazed by the consistent craftsmanship. He heard the others in the lab noting it as well even though he was trying his best to block out their irritating conversations. He had also come to a major revelation. The squares weren't the only things so similar in the lab. George, Ella, and Edward were all still the same, he could feel it. Maybe they hadn't set some elaborate trap for him, but it sure as hell wasn't a warm and welcoming return to his beloved homeland. Not that he had the slightest expectation that it would be, but he now knew he had to get the hell away from them and stay away for good. His decisions all those years ago were warranted after all and there would be no more regrets. He didn't belong with the three of them here and he never had. As painful as their statements used to be, maybe he actually had been switched at birth. The idea used to drive him so deep into himself on a regular basis that he thought he might implode. And seeing them together after all this time from the perspective of a full-grown adult, he obviously felt no different. Maybe being switched hadn't been just another cruel jab at his frequently injured heart in those days. It seemed reasonable now even to him. This trip had settled many things for good. Now he would just have to learn to deal with it, and finally make a serious effort to move on.

After some time trying to sift through the SNIU's computer records herself, the General decided their records were bordering on the work of an incompetent. Of course, that would be an insult to someone who actually was incompetent. Maybe the overwhelming extent of information and extreme ease of access her own Nation provided her at the push of a button had spoiled her. No, she decided, it was just pure incompetence. It probably still required an entire room for their system to store a gigabyte of data. Whatever its strengths, the Shawnee Nation was technologically backward. It was just another reason beyond the weather that she couldn't live there, well that and the damn bugs.

"Agent Green, do you think you could help me with this?" She finally inquired, giving in to defeat at the hands of the Shawnee Nation's primitive technology. Thirty years before in her own past, she could have flown through their current system. But that was thirty years of massive leaps in technology. The Apache Nation had outgrown the Shawnee system five minutes after it had been installed, and upgraded, upgraded at least a thousand times!

"General?" The agent said lifting his eyebrows and probably believing the system was too advanced for her instead of the extreme opposite.

"Never mind." She said, deciding it wasn't worth the effort she had already put into it, let alone more.

During the same amount of time, her com techs had gathered information from almost every other police system in the Nations. Rand needed a little advice in this area. Just because he was an ancient didn't mean his whole Nation had to flounder in the Stone Age.

"General, we have an incoming link from the Comanche Nation." One of her now unoccupied com techs said as the General continued kicking herself for having wasted so much time on the useless Shawnee system.

"Put it through." She said without a second thought. Daniels and the new sets of samples all had to be there by now, and she could seriously use a non-caffeinated boost.

Turning to the largest wall monitor, the image that took up the screen wasn't Daniels or even

Parker. It was a woman who when the General observed her carefully seemed to resemble Daniels in several ways.

"General." She said as she backed away from her own link camera, and the General was able to see the rest of the lab behind the woman. Back in the distance, and now moving quickly towards the camera, she recognized Daniels. There was no mistaking the resemblance between Daniels and the woman now.

"Captain Daniels." She said as the man came up to stand beside the woman on the screen.

The woman said, "He's here" looking behind her into the lab as she said it. The General stared in disbelief and her immediate thought was that the woman on the other end, whoever she was, could only have a brain cell or two bouncing around in her skull. Daniels was standing right beside her!

As the General continued her impromptu eyeball IQ test of the woman, two other men entered the field of view from opposite directions. General Cochise was sure that they all noticed her double take at that point. It had nearly given her whiplash, but then just as quickly cleared up a few questions still floating around in her own head about Daniels's outlandish decision to contact the enemy Comanche Nation. He unexpectedly appeared to have an identical twin brother!

"Captain?" She questioned, having been thrown off guard for the umpteenth time that day and now fearing a few more Daniels' would pop onto the screen like a sick cloning experiment gone berserk.

"Yes, General." The new arrival said loudly, stopping as far away from the other three as he could while still showing up in her monitor's field of view. He appeared tense as hell and only looked directly ahead in a stiff manner like his neck was in a cervical collar. It didn't take her gut to tell her there were some serious issues causing that gap.

"What have you gotten so far?" She asked, having difficulty not comparing the three people on the screen who weren't Council member Parker. Damn, this had certainly never occurred to her, she thought. But then how could she have known about anything as unexpected as she now saw on her monitor? Still angry about the time she had wasted, she thought well, she could have looked up Daniels's records. They now clearly had extensive biographical data on each and every one of the people on the monitor due to the Apache's careful assessment of every person in their own Nation. Parker, as a Council member, was also well researched with the information readily available to her. She had just never made this connection or anything even relatively close to it. Still kicking herself and near the point of calling herself a dumbass, she was sure the minute details of her own life hadn't similarly slipped under Parker's radar, sure in her gut at least.

"Well, first, General and Council member Cochise" Parker started, "I suspect you've been seriously underutilizing Sam's abilities."

The statement brought Captain Daniels's head turning abruptly in Parker's direction stiff neck and all, his mouth dropping open at the same time in shock and utter disbelief.

"What do you mean Council member Parker?" The General asked, her gut still churning up reflexive assessments of the now bizarre and ugly situation on the screen.

"You're Captain is nothing short of a genius." Parker smoothly went on in his politician's voice as if not noticing Captain Daniels's intense reaction to his words.

The General stood for a minute still trying to get a grasp on the smoldering intensity in the image on her monitor. Eventually back to comparing the twins at the other end of the link, she decided that captain Daniels wasn't aging nearly as well as his otherwise identical twin brother. Stress could probably do that, she surmised. Just based on his move to the Apache Nation Daniels was undoubtedly the black sheep in his family. By visually comparing the two over the link, she could tell that Daniels's status in his family had greatly impacted his life, stealing his confidence and impairing his eventual outcome. It was sad really, but none of her business.

"Well…" She finally said, not exactly sure how

to proceed after Parker's little genius bombshell.

"If you can't find a better use for him, I'm sure the Comanche Nation could." Parker continued as smooth as glass and still outwardly not acknowledging the captain's impossible to ignore responses.

Again she couldn't quite figure out what to say, and the loss of control was starting to tweak her out of her self-reproach. Parker was apparently trying to rebuild a bridge of some kind to Daniels, and she didn't know if she had anything to contribute, or if she should even try.

At that point, the woman spoke up, bringing the General's focus back to the center of the screen. "General, my name is Dr. Ella Grant, and this is my brother Dr. George Daniels. It is an honor to speak to you. We have received your samples, and have begun the analysis." She said, not changing the focus of her gaze.

"Good." The General said, interrupting Parker before he could get his next statement out.

Looking across the screen towards Daniels at last, Parker asked, "Could you possibly tell us what this is all about, General? Sam's being tight lipped on this end."

Feeling she at least had a partial grasp on the drama playing out in Parker's lab now, she responded, "Captain Daniels is at liberty to discuss this with you in full detail. It's too complicated for me to give you a thumbnail sketch over the link, Council member Parker."

"Very well then" Parker said, "Sam can catch us up, and we'll contact you again when we have some solid data." The link was abruptly terminated and the General was briefly lost in both her thoughts and in the black void of the monitor's blank screen.

As the link terminated, Ella and George turning around to see exactly what had literally been happening behind their backs. Ella had never considered that Edward would have a different opinion about how things were going with Sam in the lab. She had assumed Edward had the same feelings on the matter that she and George did. That was the way things generally went with them, they all usually thought alike.

What greeted George and Ella when they turned around was strange, if nothing else. Sam was still staring at Edward with his mouth gaping open, and Edward had just started walking over towards him.

Seeing the other two turn around, Edward said "Come on guys, let's get him into a chair or something. He's been like this for several minutes. I think he's in shock."

In concern, they all reached him at the same time and grabbed his arms to hold him up in case he started to drop out. He did manage to close his mouth, but the wide-eyed stare didn't change a bit. With a little effort, they got him to a cushioned chair along the wall, and were able to get him to sit down.

"Sam.. Sam.. are you all right?" Ella said softly as she cupped his face in both of her hands. It was going to take more than a whisper to rattle him back in to the real world.

Edward walked to a chemical storage cabinet and dabbed a cotton tipped swab into a bottle of ammonia, quickly returning with a serious look on his face. After passing the swab under Sam's nose a few times, he came out of his trance and shook his head side to side several times primarily just shaking off Ella's hands.

Sam stared in disbelief at the three people standing around him with concerned looks on their faces. It took a minute for the situation to register, but it didn't matter because he was still confused.

"What happened? Where am I?" Spilled out of his mouth quickly and then he was quiet again.

"Just calm down, Sam." George said from behind Ella. "Everything is all right." But by the time he got the words out, they didn't matter anymore.

It took a while for Sam's confusion to resolve from that point, and he continued to mostly stare up at the three of them the whole time like they were freaky aliens from another planet. After being absorbed in his unwavering stare for a short time, they moved him to a couch back in the living quarters, thinking he might feel better if he could lie down. They got him to the couch, but he

continued to sit up stiffly and look around the
room. After supporting his wobbling body on the
chair, at least they didn't have to hold him onto
the couch. They all took seats around him and
waited for him to recover from whatever had just
happened to him. It took over an hour, but he
finally began to react to his environment again.
An hour after that, he had become verbal and could
even respond to their questions.

The others' serious concern for Sam then
shifted quickly to relief that he seemed to be O.K.
The incident had broken the ice for George and Ella
like crises tend to do in families everywhere.
Edward had apparently already left them in the dust
in this regard, having deliberately caused the
crisis in the first place. It had clearly bloomed
exponentially out of his control, but Sam had
always been extremely unpredictable. Edward had
understood this decades before whereas his true
brother and sister had been unable to see him
beyond their familial difficulties regardless of
their intelligence. Sometimes it took an outsider
to see the truth. In spite of George and Ella's
unexplainable youthful treatment of their brother,
Edward knew that they had loved him just as
intensely as they effectively alienated him. There
was really no reason to it that Edward could see.
Families could be extremely irrational from what he
had observed over the years. But there was still
hope for the triplets in his mind. After all,
Sam's call had miraculously opened the way for him
to connect with the Apache Nation and Council
member Cochise. Miraculous really wasn't a strong
enough word when he considered that the Comanche
and Apache had never ever been allies throughout
their entire shared history in the Americas.

"I don't know if you caught this part or not
Sam, but General Cochise gave you permission to
fill us all in on this analysis we're doing."
Edward said after the four of them had settled into
a more comfortable frame of mind.

"No, I guess I didn't." Sam replied, a look of
confusion briefly returning to his face.

"It's O.K. Sam." Edward told him, a little
concern returning to the room.

"No, it's not O.K. I don't know what happened to me." Sam said, the confusion now mixing with worry.

"What did happen, Edward?" George asked as he shared a quick glance with Ella.

Standing up and walking back towards the lab, he said over his shoulder "We'll talk about it later. Right now we have work to do."

Sam's confusion vanished in a second, and he was the next person through the door behind Edward. Worry and confusion were meaningless in comparison to his sense of duty. He was working directly for the General and that had become something even beyond his sense of duty. With the exception of having been the person who punched him in the groin, she had been kind and maybe even friendly. At least kind and friendly in comparison to the way most other soldiers treated him. Of course, no one else had ever punched him so hard in the groin that he crumpled to the floor. Maybe it was just his sense of duty.

Casting another look at Ella, George followed the other two back into the lab and Ella returned there herself shortly later. Edward was right, they did have a considerable ways to go and they had now lost quite a few hours while they tended to Sam. Her curiosity about both Edward and Sam's behavior was probably as intense as George's, but she would wait for Edward's explanation, if he really even had one. Thinking about her own progress to that point, she decided that it was a good thing they had contacted General Cochise at a break point in the analysis. They would have all lost considerably more time if they had needed to start over from the beginning. Everything took time and she never appreciated that fact as much as when she had to repeat something because of an error.

When Ella returned to the lab she realized that Sam had fortunately already finished his prep work, and neither George nor Edward would let him do more than watch them after his catatonic episode. She understood their feelings and agreed with them. It went beyond their concern for Sam even though he was having trouble accepting their other reasons. Each of them worked in their own rhythm and were used to working alone. As much as he wanted to help, there was nothing Sam could really do that wouldn't disrupt their usual routines and possibly throw off their results. Repeating a botched experiment was painful, very painful.

As George, Ella, and Edward all recaptured their stride almost effortlessly, Sam drifted around the lab watching them work. His usual work in the Apache Nation wasn't as sophisticated, but he understood and appreciated the process. Although each of them had advanced magnitudes beyond anything he had ever done in molecular biology, the basics were unchanged. Had he stayed in the Comanche Nation, he might be near their level of expertise by now. But he hadn't and he wasn't and his earlier decision that he had no regrets was again starting to slip. George and Ella were his brother and sister after all, and it went beyond that to them being a set of triplets. He didn't know what had happened to make them so different from him and he might never know. It would never make any sense anyway. He and George were identical, and that usually resulted in a tighter than normal bond. Ella was the fraternal sibling of the triplets, but George had an unusually tight bond with her even beyond the intensity that identical twins often had. Sam had lived his entire life with a virtually nonexistent connection to either of them. When they were little and Edward had come into the picture, things had only gone down hill for Sam. By some bizarre twist of fate, Edward had essentially become the third bonded triplet. The arrangement had been unwavering to that day and at their age was undoubtedly carved in stone.

Time flew by and they eventually reached a staggered several hour wait for gel runs. All extremely hungry by this time, they retreated to the living quarters to eat and wait out the electrophoresis of the samples. Even with three full kitchens in the living quarters and a large stock of supplies, fast and easy won out so they ordered food. The wait was short and they were

soon full and lounging back in Edward's living room
to wait out the remainder of the gel runs.

With the decades long gap between them now
narrowing, Ella sat down next to Sam on the couch
and held onto his hand with both of hers. Although
slightly taken aback, he didn't resist and they
were all soon chattering about their progress.
With over two hundred gels now running, the lab
looked like a factory more than anything else.
There were probably few labs in the Nations with as
much capacity and far fewer with people adept
enough to manage so much at one time. They didn't
usually run this high of a volume, but they had in
the not too distant past and the sight was
impressive to anyone who knew any better, Sam
included.

"We're glad you're here, Sam." Edward said
after the lab chatter settled down.

Sam looked around at the other three people in
the room and both George and Ella nodded in
agreement.

"Speaking of that, Edward, what happened
earlier?" George asked with a shift to a more
serious look.

"Well.." Edward began, "I've been thinking a
lot lately." But he was cut off immediately by
George saying, "Wow, you've been thinking?"

Before Edward could call George a smartass for
the six billionth time in their lives, Sam was
laughing so hard that the rest of them couldn't do
anything but laugh with him. It took a little
while before they all settled back down and then
everyone quietly looked at each other with smiles
on their faces.

When her curiosity peaked again, Ella said,
"Really now Edward, tell us what happened back in
the lab."

"It's not that I planned for it to go that
way," Edward started again, "but I wanted Sam to
feel welcome, and expressing it to General Cochise
seemed like a way to do it. Things were tense
before that, but I never expected it to push him
into shock."

George and Ella looked at Edward for a while,
and then turned to see Sam staring at the floor,

tears returning to his eyes, but this time not due to laughter.

Looking back to Edward, Sam asked, "Did you mean what you said?"

Now looking back at the other three very seriously, Edward answered. "It's horrible that things have gotten so bad that you even have to ask that Sam, but yes...absolutely."

Tilting his head to stare at the floor again, Sam's tears flowed freely and Ella let go of his hand to give him a big hug. She was crying now too.

"Is that all it was?" George asked Edward.

Still serious, Edward answered, "I guess so. I was trying not to look at him when I started off. The General was on the screen you know."

George said softly, "Was she, I didn't catch that part." And they all started laughing again. The decades of separation had melted away at last, and when the laughter stopped again, Ella felt very comfortable in asking Sam about the work they were doing.

"I don't know a whole lot," he started, "but I'll tell you what I know. It all started for me after they found the sergeant's body in the desert."

"Ah, the reason for the emergency Council meeting," Edward said calmly, "I sort of suspected that."

"Yes, from what I understand."

"But what could those tiny squares of bone have to do with a murder?" Ella asked, mentally trying to assess the few facts she now had to work with.

"That's still one of the major questions. Have you told George and Ella about the sergeant?" Sam asked Edward now, trying to see how far back he needed to start.

"Some of the major points." He started. "Primarily that she was murdered, scalped and left in a burial ground."

"The bone fragments were found under her body and buried just below the surface." Sam then said.

"O.K., so they found pieces of bone in a burial ground. That's like finding water in the ocean." George commented, receiving a smirk from Ella for his effort.

"That's what I would have thought, and I might still think that except for a few significant things." Sam said, not offended by George at all. "The first thing that pulled my thinking away from them being random grave remnants was the shape. They have all been perfect squares to this point and identical in size to the micron."

"Well, that makes them unusual I guess," Edward said, "but they are still pieces of bone from a burial ground."

"I know, but I can't see why anyone would take the time to craft them. They have definitely been crafted by my observations." Sam replied.

"But people do stupid, pointless things every day, Sam. It's not like they're moon rocks. They're still little pieces of bone from a graveyard." George stated, this time without receiving any dirty looks from Ella.

"Yeh, I know. And again that could carry over to them all being buried edge up and at the same depth in the soil, but only below the body. None of those facts are overtly bizarre."

"Precise placement could just be expected from a person who would go to the trouble of making them in the first place." Ella said now.

"Those are all just details really," Sam returned, "and they are interesting points that developed in the first find. They become much more significant when the identical setup is found in another Nation, also under a scalped dead body."

The room became very quiet with Sam's last statement. He saw the other three sitting unmoving and knew that each of them was racing through the implications.

"To make it easier, the bone chips have now been found below several other bodies in the Shawnee Nation. You've seen them. They're exactly the same in every set."

"That's why they were boxed separately?" George asked, knowing the answer even before he asked.

"Precisely!" Sam said as he watched them fly to the appropriate conclusions in seconds.

"A serial killer.." Ella said, letting out a long breath she had apparently been holding as she thought.

With her last words, the first timer went off in the lab and a second one followed it quickly. All four of them jumped up and went back into the lab. The electrophoresis was terminated in each gel as the timers went off and the gels were placed in individual stain trays to soak. There would be another wait when the gels were all soaking up stain, but they all had more to think and talk about while they waited.

When they were all sitting back in Edward's living room for the next wait, the questions began to fly. They weren't just directed at Sam now, but to anyone else with any thoughts down the same line. The conversation went on excitedly for the entire staining period, in fact they prolonged the staining time to accommodate their brainstorming. They still didn't know what to expect from the analysis or how the results would even be helpful.

CHAPTER 12

Following the link with Parker's lab, the General settled down in front of a console to browse through data from other Nations' crime logs. Nothing absolute had popped up in relation to the killer's MO, but like the Cherokee Nation death, the details of a similar murder could be buried in otherwise incomplete or inaccurate information. The first thing she noticed was as she had expected. There hadn't been a death associated with a scalping in any of the Nations for as far back as the records went, and that was a couple of centuries in some cases.

After a coffee break, she searched for any prior case in which small squares of bone had been left at the scene. Since every square they had found to date had been buried, the chances of pulling anything similar out of the Nations' records was probably in the magnitudes of zero range, but she looked anyway.

Her scan of missing persons in the Shawnee Nation by way of one of her com techs wasn't very revealing for the local area, but showed increased reports in many other areas of the Nation. With so many bodies clustered here in this small area, it was likely they could be the missing local people, but the useful data had to be in hard copies somewhere in the region because it continued to not be in the SNIU's horrible computer records. This helped validate her belief about the Shawnee Nation and technology, but also represented another waste of time on her part and this led to her negative thoughts starting to creep back in. She could protect herself from that kind of torment by heading out into the crappy weather. It almost sounded fun in comparison, so she pulled on rain gear this time and went in search of captain Atwell and the last of the dig sites.

The first obvious thing she noticed as she opened the mobile command center door was a decrease in the size of the media camp. With no information leaking from her soldiers and only two SNIU agents out there in the farm field some of the local station crews had given up and pulled out. A couple of others were buried axle deep in mud and were still trying to get out of the field. The General smiled and leapt off the stairs into the muddy field. Her command center would pull them out in the long run if necessary. It would make good press for the Apache Nation as the crews that weren't stuck filmed them in the process.

All of the canvas shells were still up and had held through the storm, but the bright lights inside now lighted up only a few. Captain Atwell had to be in one of them so she walked towards the farthest one believing he would be in the last one she checked so she might as well get the longest walk out of the way. As she came up to the mid-distance tent, she heard the captain talking inside. Her life still had some balance it seemed, so she smiled and went inside. The site crew had excavated most of the area enclosed by the canvas because the scatter pattern had been intense but also large. They had already recovered a set of bone chips from the dig, but had proceeded beyond

147

that point to cover the whole area. The team was down nearly a foot by the tent flap so she almost took a nosedive into the giant hole as she came through. Captain Atwell was standing near the flap and fortunately helped her catch her balance after her unexpected drop.

"Sorry, General. Didn't expect any visitors." leapt out of the captain's mouth before he had time to think about it.

The General gave the captain and the site crew a quick glance and said, "Thank you, captain," as her instantaneous irritation from the near fall vanished almost as quickly as it had swelled up. The smile that had crept onto her face just before she came through the tent flap returned immediately afterwards as she surveyed the massive amount of work the team had done.

"Are you digging a basement for the tent, captain?" then came out of the General's mouth as she decided not to filter it out.

The captain looked around straight faced and said, "No Sir, just being thorough."

The crew continued working on as the captain then gave his full attention to the General.

"It was a joke, captain," She eventually replied as he remained straight-faced and nearly but not quite at attention. "At ease."

The captain loosened up a little, saying, "Yes Sir." almost automatically in the process.

The General continued to smile and said, "That's an order, captain." as she sensed his tension level had barely decreased.

Reluctantly, the captain relaxed further and began to observe the site crew again.

"This is good work, captain." She then said.

"Yes it is," he answered, and then went on to say "it was like this when I got here."

Seeing the entire crew give the captain a quick look, she was pretty sure that it hadn't been. The General gave the captain a short assessment, smiling the whole time and then congratulated the crew for their work. The captain then actually smiled and she decided he was a good man on the spot. There wouldn't be any psych evals for the captain. He had it together and didn't need to ride on the backs of others to gain some fleeting and hollow glory. He was a good leader, one she could relate to, and he would do well in his career.

Before she could ask, the captain said, "The other crews are finishing up, Sir." and with that she also heard the rain stop its little taps on the canvas above her.

"I'm outa here." She said as she turned and took the step up out of the tent. The rain was still dropping a little from the trees, but it had otherwise stopped. Skipping the farthest dig, she still checked in on the site closest to the command center. They had been slowed down considerably by the root system of a tree they had cut down to erect their tent. If she had come across something similar in the Cherokee Nation, she would have immediately walked away. Her easy dig had been bad enough. She wondered if the captain had pushed this crew as well as the last one. He of course would never say, but it was another damn good job.

After the General ditched her mud boots and rain gear, she reentered the command center, stopping before she closed the door to observe the media camp. It looked like they would be pulling out quite a few news vans before they left the area. Rand would be proud. She then wondered if he had ever used an electric winch, but decided against it in favor of him having used a mammoth or a mastodon. Those animals should have had some pretty good pulling power back in his day. The smile remained on her face as she closed the door.

The command center was amazingly quiet for the number of people it now held. The only thing disturbing the peace seemed to be the SNIU agents' squawky old radios. She might have had a Middle East flashback if the Apache Nation military had been using such crappy technology at the time. She didn't have flashbacks from her childhood, but if she did the sounds would probably fit.

The squawking abruptly worsened and was unfortunately serenaded by one of the SNIU agents as he nearly yelled to override the static. The yelling quickly ended, but the squawking continued intermittently. The General walked over and took a seat in front of their monitor sized site map to look it over for one last time. They had predicted hits pretty effectively and there weren't any other areas that she was even slightly concerned about. Her thoughts drifted to the analysis being done in Parker's lab and she had an urge to contact them, but was rudely interrupted when one of the SNIU agents standing right beside her started yelling loudly to someone on one of their primitive radios. She needed to talk to Rand about current technology. The SNIU and probably his entire Nation could use a monumental tech infusion.

The squawking and yelling continued for a few minutes and then stopped again. After giving the SNIU agent a dirty look, the General refocused on the site map in front of her. She stared at it a few seconds before her thoughts cleared enough for her to remember she was done with the map. Before she could consider anything else, the SNIU radio was going off again and the racket seemed to vibrate her brain. This time she could pick up more from the horrible noise, and the SNIU agent didn't have to yell quite as loud.

From what she could pick up through the static, the two SNIU agents were on the verge of being pulled from her investigation to an active search for missing children not far from their current location. She decided that the short distance between the communicators accounted for the 'clarity' in the communications this time. The searchers were reportedly desperate for manpower, but most of the SNIU agents were pretty well scattered around the Shawnee Nation from what she could hear. Through all of the background noise, the situation there still sounded tense. It had to be bad there for her to be able to pick up the tension. The agents out in the farm field with her were comparatively close to the search location though and would most likely be pulled from her to assist in the search. The first thought that came to the General's mind was that she would be spared from the continued SNIU radio noise. Her brain was still vibrating from the past several bouts of squawking and if she had to endure it any longer she might throw the SNIU radios in the toilet.

The agent closest to the General then advised her that they would be leaving. She felt a little irritated by the SNIU move, but not as irritated as the radios were making her. In fact, she wasn't upset about them being pulled at all, it was just the radios getting to her. She understood the reasons behind the move and she would have done the same thing under similar circumstances.

Even after several calls the SNIU agents weren't in any hurry to leave the command center. The horrible squawking flared up again a few time before the General could partially make out another transmission. The situation near there had gotten a little worse when the SNIU had picked up a murder case in addition to the missing boys. A second investigation in the town now involved a man who had been brutally attacked and then died shortly afterwards. They needed more help already, so when they shifted some of their scarce agents over to the murder, they would be in serious trouble. Still irritated by the radio squawking, she decided the agents needed to leave before she lost it and threw the agents in the toilet along with their noise boxes.

It was at that very point while she was still thinking bad thoughts that Agent Green asked if she could spare some soldiers to aid in the search. Amazed by his nerve at first, she reined in her irritation and sat down to analyze her current needs at the farm field dig site. They were winding down at the site after all, and some of her crews were already struggling with boredom, or so it seemed. Thinking in those terms, it didn't take long before she offered the help of three of her crews. It wouldn't be their usual line of detail work, but she was sure they could lend a hand in the search if nothing else. The search wouldn't last forever.

Quickly rethinking the situation before her three forensic crews could move out, she felt her own Apache urge to be mobile return with a vengeance. She had been out at the site in the farm field for too damn long. She could leave Atwell to close out the dig site. Then she could travel the supposedly short distance to Hawthorne with her

soldiers to assist the SNIU. She would set it up
with the captain and also authorize him to pull any
news vans out that were still stuck in the field.
She would then have the rest of her teams meet her
in Hawthorne to assist in the search if it was
still necessary. It was amazing that the SNIU
could coordinate anything with their ancient
equipment anyway, so with the addition of the
General and twelve of her soldiers, communications
would be dramatically improved.

Thinking deeper, the General's Council self
took over and she decided a little effort on her
part might make an impact on Rand and give her more
political pull if needed in the Eastern Council.
It hadn't ever mattered up to that point, but that
didn't mean it wouldn't matter in the future. Rand
obviously had a massive amount of power in his
Nation and she needed to keep that in perspective.
But as she thought about Rand she couldn't help but
think that she must respect and assist her elders,
or ancients in his particular case. Respect or
not, she then also realized she needed to stop the
'ancient' references before she accidentally said
something along that line when Rand was around to
hear her. That would undoubtedly send her
political influence in the Eastern Intertribal
Council into the toilet. Toilets were for SNIU
radios and the agents who toted them around. She
needed to watch her thoughts and especially keep
her mouth in line.

A half an hour later, the General had briefed
captain Atwell and was confident he could manage
the site when she left to join the search. The
forensic teams had already dismantled most of the
tents and were packing them under the command
center even though they were wet; not truly wet,
because they were polymer treated and they shed
water like they had been coated in grease. They
would still need a little attention when the
command center returned to the St. Louis, Sioux
Nation Apache base.

When the general authorized the captain to
pull the news vans out of the field, he couldn't
help but smile. Like almost everyone else who
served under her, he knew she hated the media. He

didn't know how valid it was, but the rumors that had filtered down over the past two decades were so well known that they might as well be fact. He had already witnessed her evade the media like the plague on a few occasions and he had rarely been under her direct command.

With the captain's broad smile, the General had difficulty controlling her own gloating feelings and she eventually cracked a big smile herself. She was bending over backwards to help the slimy media weasels and whether this particular bunch of vermin knew it or not, they didn't deserve her assistance and they never would. If she ever got absolute confirmation of her beliefs, the media would be keeping their distance from her and then only if she even allowed them to exist.

Still smiling, the General took the driver's seat of the Jaagé she had arrived in with captain Atwell. It took a little while for the soldiers who couldn't fit in the other Jaagés her teams were taking to get up enough nerve to reluctantly climb in with her, but she did eventually get two takers. By shying away from her, they made things worse when they both took seats in the back. Her smile not fading even then, she made a huge shrug that the captain had to see and cranked the Jaagés engine. He continued to smile as she pulled away through the muddy field and looked back at him in her rear view mirror. He was a good officer and she was going to make sure he was promoted after all they had been through. He had gone above and beyond her expectations of him and that wasn't exactly an easy thing to do. Soldiers had been promoted for a hell of a lot less and she would push the system until it did what was appropriate. In reality, there would be no resistance. The General was well known to avoid the political aspects of requesting promotions and this hadn't changed when she joined the Intertribal Council. Her request would be honored immediately and with great fanfare. In spite of her own feelings for the media, the Apache Nation viewed them as a tool that was used and abused as they saw fit. The Nation's relationship with the media had always been like that, and it was part of the reason she despised the media as much as she did.

When the General pulled out of the field and onto the poorly kept Shawnee Nation road, her thoughts about the media faded like the winding road behind her. As much of a pessimist as she was, dwelling on the contingent that had nearly destroyed her life wouldn't get her anywhere. With a number of corrupt outside factors involved, she would never have the proof she needed. As powerful as the Apache Nation and the Intertribal Council were, there were still sinister powers working against them that were equally powerful. Their power wasn't subject to public scrutiny however, so they wielded it viciously, and in the darker corners of the world, working against them was as good as a death sentence. Not bound by law or even honor, they were capable of anything, and the Nations' recent history was full of the evidence of their workings. The media made sure of it, thriving on the chaos and perpetuating it like only they were capable of doing. It was a symbiotic relationship between two parasites, a relationship the General would love to take down. She tolerated the discomfort of being on the Council for that reason and for that reason only. Eventually it would pay off for her, and she was waiting for that day.

The captain watched as the General ripped through the muddy field in her Jaagé following the other three Jaagés that had already moved out. He then looked over at the half-dozen news vans still stuck in the mud and chuckled a little to himself. There was only one forensic crew that hadn't broken down their site and he would have to give them the O.K. to stop digging. He imagined the tree roots were a nightmare and the team could be stuck there for days if he pushed them to keep searching. They had already found a set of bone chips at the beginning of their dig, but he had encouraged them to go wider just in case. Of course they had only gone on to find frustration, but they had gone on with the work as he had requested.

Turning away from the stuck vehicles, he walked around the command center and went directly to the only remaining tent. As he pulled back the

154

flap, he saw that the crew was still meticulously clearing and cleaning the root system. They still hadn't found anything since the initial set of bone squares.

"Let's close up shop." He said as they turned to see who had come in.

It would be a little while before they had everything packed away, but he had a few other things to tend to. The command center needed to be made road ready and then there was the news people to deal with. In all likelihood, a Jaagé could pull them out and he wouldn't have to wait until the command center was in position with its winch.

When he returned to the command center, he ordered another forensic team to assist in the breakdown of the last tent. He then ordered two other teams to work on digging the media wagons out of the field. The soldiers stared at him for a second and he knew what they were thinking.

"It's a specific request from the General." He said in an explanation he didn't really have to give.

His statement only prolonged the stare for a few seconds and then the soldiers were out the door. He could hear them chattering before the door closed. The rumors about the General were universally known and generally easily understood by the soldiers in the Apache Nation.

What he and most other people had heard was that the media was in some way responsible for the death of the General's husband back in the Middle East War. Like they were frequently allowed to do back then from what he understood, the NNS had embedded a reporter in her husband's unit. It was extremely common and the General herself probably had one in her own unit at the time. The Apache Nation had once encouraged it basically as publicity to promote the Nation's military effectiveness and therefore gain more contracts for their services. In essence, it was business and business can be as ruthless as war. This was particularly true in the Apache Nation's case when it came to their military. As the sole financial foundation of the Nation, serious self-promotion had once been seen as a necessity. It still had its benefits and the Nation continued to have extensive interactions with the media. The relationship was no longer as reckless as it had been though and the soldiers all knew this had only come about after the Nation lost the General's husband and his unit in the war. There had never been absolute proof, or at least none that the Nation allowed to exist after the fact, but the almost universal belief was that the imbedded NNS reporter had somehow leaked the unit's position and compromised their mission. The true cause may have been plausibly deniable, but the end result sure as hell wasn't. Her husband's unit had been ambushed and wiped out so quickly that they probably never knew what hit them. The journalist hadn't been with them on the mission for some reason that was difficult for him to explain away afterwards, but the media monsters protected him like he was a hero who had miraculously survived his unit's destruction. He had survived all right, but it was far from a miracle. The initial investigation had hinted at the true cause, but had abruptly been shut down. By the time anyone was able to investigate why it had been terminated; any evidence that would have led to the cause was reportedly not to be found. The captain had only been a kid at the time, but he remembered it like every other Apache who had been alive during the Middle East War. He could still see the image of the General on the news back then, although she was younger and a captain at the time. She had pushed for more to be done, but she didn't have the power then that she had as both a General and a Council member currently, and the event had faded into the past for most people outside of their Nation.

The captain ordered the remaining soldiers to ready the mobile command center to move out and then got to work himself stowing away anything that they had used while there that wasn't nailed down. There wasn't much, but order was the military way and it was never worth the risk of coming across a higher-ranking officer in a really bad mood.

They were actually road ready in a few minutes with most of the command center's components being automated. The jumbo tires on the rig then pulled

the command center out of the muddy field like it
was an empty cardboard box. The Jaagés weren't
doing as well with a couple of the media vans, the
news crews having buried them even deeper in a
frantic effort to follow the General earlier as she
whipped out of the field. The soldiers were now to
the point of using two Jaagés at a time to drag the
last vans out and the first media crews to be
pulled out were laughing and filming the spectacle
like they had never been stuck themselves. With
the power of two military Jaagés in tandem
potentially capable of ripping a van in half, the
event was pretty entertaining to the soldiers as
well and it was over before they had gotten a
chance to enjoy it enough. What they were heading
to would be light duty though, so they were still
happy as they hit the old road in route to the
search.

CHAPTER 13

The drive to the little Shawnee Nation town of
Hawthorne only took a half an hour, but felt longer
because they had to slow down frequently for sharp
curves in the old road. It seemed to the General
at times that the road had been made to curve
around every tree that stood in its way. The roads
were different in the desert. She would be back
there soon.

When she hit the outskirts of the town, she
was amused to see people standing in their yards
watching them like the few military Jaagés were a
parade. The town had been carved out of the
Shawnee Forest and was molded to the hills in the
area like a wet piece of cloth. Some people would
have described it as quaint, but the General wasn't
one of those people. Except for one clothing store
they passed on the main road through town, the
place was about as lively as a morgue. It would
take a strange breed of people to live there and
she was glad she wouldn't be there long.

The small caravan of Jaagés crept through the
town behind the SNIU vehicle that had caught up to

on the way and were soon pulling off the road near
what she initially thought was a tree lined field.
The General didn't realize that the field was the
lawn of some large dark building set back pretty
far from the road until she climbed out of the
Jaagé and looked around. The whole area was lit by
the multistrobe effect of numerous police car
lights scattered around the perimeter of the
property. Every police car in the town along with
any the SNIU had scraped up had to already be
there, and the situation was obviously writhing in
chaos.

The arrival of the four Apache military Jaagés
caught the attention of the local law enforcement
like it had the town people along the road, and
every one of them stood whispering and staring like
little children.

Great, the General thought, they were the new
dog and pony show in town. The locals would be too
busy gawking to be of any help and she didn't know
a damn thing about the stupid little town. The
stares intensified as she and her soldiers strapped
on their weapons and stood around the Jaagés like
they were piles of lost Inca gold. The two SNIU
agents that had been with them in the farm field
finally crawled out of their vehicle and she
watched as they swaggered over to what had to be
their SNIU cohorts. Within seconds they were also
all gawking at the soldiers and it appeared to the
General that the supposed search had just switched
off like a dim and dying little bulb. This
wouldn't do, this wouldn't do at all, she thought
immediately and motioned for two of her soldiers to
follow her over to the SNIU agents she was already
thinking of as boys. Unlike the Shawnee Nation
medical examiner, these 'boys' were nearing her own
age and some were probably even older. But the
attitudes and lack of discipline were juvenile, and
she would prefer that they just stayed the hell out
of her way. She had come there with her soldiers
to take care of business and if she had to take
over for it to be done right, so be it.

On reaching the agents with her two Apache
soldiers in her wake, she immediately addressed one
of the agents who had been at the dig site, the one

in particular who had insinuated that she was incapable of using a computer.

"Agent Green," she began in a curt and commanding voice that practically brought the agents to attention. Military wanna-bes, she thought. They had probably all washed out and fled back to the Shawnee Nation to pick up SNIU jobs, all of them except Green of course who now responded to her the same way he had in the command center. He was an idiot who didn't realize he was an idiot, dangerous on the battlefield and a pain in the ass to deal with on a good day. Knowing his measure already, she didn't waste time with him.

"We have limited time, but you have our services. We need to get to it and find these kids."

Agent Green looked at her with his continued bad attitude, but he wasn't the senior agent at the scene and a slightly older man with the stance of someone who had at least made it through boot camp spoke up.

"General Cochise, I'm agent Rivers. I'm in command of the search at this point and I gratefully accept your assistance." As he said this he glanced at agent Green with a look that told him to back off, and then said, "I can brief you on the situation unless agent Green has already done so."

Without looking back at Green, she said, "I would appreciate the information, Agent Rivers. We are here to help you and anything you can tell us that will allow us to help you in the most efficient way will be valuable."

Agent Rivers now glanced back at agent Green with a look that said stand back you incompetent idiot, and immediately began to describe the situation to the General. Green needed a serious reprimand for his arrogant disregard for the General's status in the Nations, the Shawnee Nation included. He would deal with that later. Council member Rand had spoken to Rivers directly when the General had entered the Shawnee Nation. Rand was not someone you crossed. People who had crossed him in the past left the Nation, and they always left no matter who they were.

As Agent Rivers discussed the case with the

General, she caught the arrival of several news
vans out of the corner of her eye. The parasites
had trailed them to the town. The sooner they got
this over with the better. In a situation not
controlled by her military, they would run rampant
and she couldn't tolerate that even on reportedly
private property in another Nation. The locals
wouldn't and couldn't understand.

But then Agent Rivers surprised her in the way
that most positive things in her pessimistic life
surprised her. He ordered the other SNIU agents to
tape off the area and keep the reporters both away
and in the dark in terms of their progress in the
search. While he was doing this she noticed
something she rarely saw outside of her own Nation.
The agent had the emblem of the Apache military
inscribed in black across the back of his right
hand. He had served in the Middle East War as an
Apache soldier. The insignia was universally
inscribed in that way for that war and only that
war. Looking at the back of her own right hand,
memories of the war crept back and she felt a
respectful bond to Agent Rivers. He had been there
and somehow ended up in the Shawnee Nation as an
SNIU agent afterwards. It hadn't been uncommon
after the war for converts from other Nations to
return to their premilitary roots. The war had
been brutal and altered people in ways not seen in
the Apache military before that or at least not to
that extent. She knew there were soldiers like
Agent Rivers scattered across the Nations, but she
had never met one since the war. She rarely
interacted with people outside of her own Nation
before she joined the Intertribal Council, and the
Council didn't put her in direct contact with
people like Agent Rivers. When she looked back up
from her own hand, she saw the agent looking at her
with an expression indicating he understood and
respected her loss.

When he had finished directing the other SNIU
agents and any local law enforcement officers
capable of following an order, Agent Rivers
returned to briefing the General on the search.
The SNIU had been involved in the case of the
missing boys for days already, but the phone call

they had gotten earlier that day was the only break they had gotten in the case to that point. The tip had come from a kid, so doubts about its validity had swelled up quickly in some peoples' minds.

A flurry of activity a little ways down the road then briefly caught their attention, but they returned to their discussion and the General had been fully briefed soon after that. The search was confined to the area around the old building, and the old building was a funeral home, a dead house in her eyes. Like most other things associated with the dead, she had an initial impulse to get away and stay away from the building. She had never once entered a dead house and she didn't plan on making this a first time. Assisting in the search was one thing, but overriding her lifelong beliefs to do so was beyond what she was readily willing to do. If the boys were to be found in there, they would be found without her taking a single step inside.

With a quick glance at the dead house, the General returned to the Jaagés and her soldiers. They would all need a little gearing up before starting the search. Fortunately, they were all members of forensics teams and had no difficulty with the dead. She was the one who needed to work herself up for the search just to stay out by the road.

Not long after returning to the Jaagés, Agent Rivers led a civilian woman and a uniformed local policeman over to her and began to explain the woman's request. The woman lived in the town and had for most of her life. She had been a local realtor's secretary until recently and had knowledge of the dead house since it had been for sale for quite a few years. She was willing to enter and actually requesting the opportunity to assist in the search of the dead house. If nothing else, she was crazy and the General began to weigh the benefits of the crazy local woman's knowledge of the dead house layout against the likelihood that she would snap and endanger her soldiers or anyone else.

Before she could think it over, she saw the mobile command center coming towards her from down

the street. Her remaining soldiers were escorting
it in the rest of the Jaagés that had been in the
field. There were unfortunately a few media vans
tailing them as well and she guessed that they were
the ones her soldiers had pulled out of the field.
No good deed goes unpunished, she thought bitterly.
What she did in the name of politics sometimes
turned her stomach.

The General stared back at the woman for a
minute and then decided that if she was crazy
enough to want to go into the dead house, the woman
might spare a couple of her soldiers from having to
go in just by the time her knowledge of the layout
could save them. If she hadn't had so much
difficulty with the idea of going in there herself,
she would never have considered sending the woman
in. Of course, if Green had informed her of where
they would be searching, they also probably
wouldn't be there. Forensic crews or not, she
didn't believe in sending people to do something
she wouldn't do herself. In this case, and since
they were already at the dead house, she would at
least give her soldiers the benefit of the woman's
knowledge, or so she told herself as she nodded the
O.K. She would probably regret it later, but it
was done now.

Turning abruptly and walking away towards the
mobile command center, the General instructed
captain Atwell to make the command center usable
and then stood and watched as it was quickly done.
They would use the radio system inside to monitor
the search of the dead house and collect any
further information about it that they could before
she sent her people in there.

Following a very short wait, the General
climbed into the command center and requested a
search for data on the dead house. The results
were quick because there was very little documented
about the place beyond property ownership. There
was nothing of value to assist them in the search,
but there were a few reports of deaths occurring in
there as opposed to the people being brought in
already dead. These were primarily deaths of
people within the owner's family, a Marcus Lemont.
Again, not helpful but more reasons for her to stay

out.

In spite of his long line Apache roots, captain Atwell would lead the search into the dead house. With a little bit of luck, it would be quick and he would be out before he knew it. Maybe luck tended to fall on his side of the fence unlike her experience with it. With that less than positive thought, the General took a seat next to her com tech and began the wait for the search to begin.

But sitting inactive was never good for the General and bad thoughts began to flow through her head almost immediately. First of all, even though at its foundation she knew it was a mistake, the General would still allow the civilian woman to go along for the search of the dead house. Her Supposed knowledge of the place's layout wouldn't normally have meant a damn thing. But in this unusual case, with the funeral home being a house of the dead and also having something of a reputation as a mysterious life taker, her Apache beliefs held strange dominion over reason. Under this type of reasoning, anyone who was crazy and actually wanted to go into the dead house was something of an asset under circumstances where even her best Apache soldiers of long blood lines would have serious reservations. Since the town Hawthorne was a relatively recent immigrant community, the current residents of the area barely had native roots. But even they were reportedly terrified of the place. After she had bypassed the useless local records completely, she had found that the thorough Apache records documented evidence of some abnormal events occurring in the place including the unexplained deaths of the previous owners while in there. It didn't take her deeply held Apache beliefs or even her gut feelings to warn her of the danger in the place.

When finally ready and with the dead house lit brighter than a baseball stadium, the General authorized her soldiers to enter through the front door and they did so with military precision. The woman who had practically begged the General to let her go was soon trying desperately to keep up with the pack and quickly found herself at the base of

163

the massive staircase staring at a pool of dried
blood on the floor. An image of the man the woman
had picked up at a party filled her thoughts for a
moment until she was pushed aside by two Apache
soldiers on their way up. The woman panicked, the
man might still be up there, DEAD!

"Hey, uhh... you'd better let me go up first,"
she muttered quickly. "We need to miss the rotten
steps." She then managed to spit out hoping they
would buy her ridiculous line without question.

Amazingly, the soldiers stopped in mid-step
and dropped behind her without a word. The General
had sent her in with them because she knew the
place. Besides, they all knew the woman had to be
crazy or stupid to volunteer. It didn't matter to
them as long as they all made it back out alive.

Irrationally thinking that things were still
going good and in her favor, the woman grabbed the
opportunity before either she or the soldiers had
more time to think about it. She had already
decided that deep thinking wasn't and couldn't be a
big part of her venture, so she continued to move
forward driven purely by impulse as she practically
ran up the stairs

Pretending to acknowledge the presence of her
fabricated danger, she skipped a couple of steps
near the top on another impulse. Keeping her
advantage, she ignored the soldiers behind her and
moved down the hall immediately after reaching the
second floor. If the guy from the party was dead
up there she thought, she had to be the first one
to get to him. It definitely wasn't a rational
thought, but in her continued panic it seemed
strangely urgent. When she reached the first door,
she paused for a moment to look farther down the
hall. The soldiers behind her were seriously
taping off the top steps before they went on.
Turning back the other way, she saw that the hall
was empty as far down as she could see. If the guy
had been attacked he must have crawled into a room
or something. He could have gotten out of there of
course like she did, but she hadn't heard anything
on the news about him or seen him around. Of
course she wasn't a big fan of the local news and
she had barely left her house since that night, so

it was a pretty meaningless thought. Thinking just wasn't necessary.

Still alone, she pulled the first door open only to find that the stupid closet behind it looked pretty empty to her so she quickly moved on. The next door only a few feet down the hall also opened to reveal an empty closet and was hardly worth the horrible tension that was now building as she moved down the hall. Her two wasteful delays had given two soldiers time to make it over and stand directly behind her by then. Looking past her and blocking her from traveling further down the hall, one of the soldiers flashed a light quickly through the small doorway, and the intense light revealed a dull dark patch on the floor she hadn't noticed before in the dark. Immediately stooping down to examine the closet floor, the soldier stumbled over her foot as she tried to back out of his way. A second later, he was gone. Both the woman and the other soldier stared in disbelief at the again empty closet. The only indication that he had ever even been there was a few scratch marks through the dark patch on the floor. The woman thought she was really losing it and blinked really hard several times to try and bring him back.

The other soldier recovered immediately and called for assistance as he looked back toward the stairs. He stayed at the woman's side as horrible thoughts began to pass through her head. Her resolve wavered for a second and then a swarm of additional soldiers flew up the stairs skipping the marked last two and they all surrounded the door to the still vacant closet. The soldier who had called for help used the barrel of his weapon to probe the closet floor, and it gave way with very little effort, popping down and back up like it was spring loaded. A trap door, they had found a trap door!

Before anyone could grab her, the woman impulsively stuck her foot on the panel and it swung down all the way with her weight. Off balance, she fell through the hole, and was out of sight before the soldiers knew it.

The General had heard the call for help over
the radios and sat tensely waiting for an
explanation. When nothing was said for a few
seconds, she asked, "Captain Atwell, what's your
status?"

The captain responded immediately with, "We
just lost two people, General, the woman and
corporal Garner."

"What?" She replied, "What the hell happened?"

"They fell through a trap door, Sir. We're
going down to check it out." He replied crisply,
remaining calm in spite of the bizarre and
unexpected event.

Once through the trap door, the sensation of
falling swept over the woman. This was it...she
was going to die like a crazy idiot, managed to fly
through her mind like she was falling in slow
motion. But the landing was soft, or at least,
soft for her. It was too dark for her to know for
sure, but it felt like she had landed on another
person. Whatever it was, it had probably saved her
life. A sudden burst of light from the trap door
thirty feet above her brought the whole sickening
scene vividly to her eyes. The twisted body of the
soldier lay beneath her along with several others
in a rotten stinking mass of flesh. Her stomach
churned violently and she threw up before she could
get off of the pile. Bile filled her nose and only
added to the stench. Still choking, she watched as
several soldiers scurried down the ladder bolted to
the far side of the shaft she had just plunged
through. She had been damn lucky to miss it. The
soldier hadn't been as fortunate, and by the looks
of it, neither had a few others. The room was
starting to fill with soldiers by that time, most
trying desperately to miss the dead soldier topped
disgusting pile of rotting humans lying in their
paths at the base of the ladder. Aside from the
soldier, the only discernible figures were of what
looked like two small boys, both bloating and
already nearly unrecognizable. The soldier lay on
top of them and would have survived the fall if it
hadn't been for the ladder. It was the obvious
explanation for the fact that his head had almost

broken clear of his spine. At least it had been a quick death for him, the woman thought. It was impossible to even guess how long the others had suffered after the fall and before they died.

As one of the first soldiers down the ladder, captain Atwell took in the rotting mass at his feet. Garner was as dead as he would ever get and it looked like they might have found the lost boys.

Choosing to be brief and blunt in his report, he said, "General, we've got three dead here, Garner and probably our missing boys."

"How?" She asked tensely over the radio.

"The fall, Sir, it has to be at least thirty feet."

"What about the woman? You said three dead, right?" She asked, her voice tight. She had just lost a soldier on this stupid little escapade and she was already swimming in black thoughts.

"She's here, Sir, alive and apparently uninjured." He responded as he looked across the small room at her. Comparing her to the mangled form of Garner, he decided the woman had to be half cat.

The General was silent. The darkness had swallowed her and she just stared at the console in front of her.

Through with her retching and choking, the woman was already scanning the rest of the room. A large red brick wall immediately caught her attention. It stood out dramatically from the rest of the room, which was made entirely of light grey cement blocks. Jumping to her feet, she fought back the nausea again and ran to the wall. This had to be the place! Nothing else she had seen before in the funeral home came close to matching the translations on the old manuscripts.

Captain Daniels helped the others as they drained the stain off of the gels and prepared to start the washes in well over two hundred containers spread out through the lab. The analysis had gone amazingly fast considering his episode, but they did have the best equipment available there and an abundance of it. They were

167

also as good as their reputations, and he felt the
beginnings of an unusual feeling stir in him. What
was it, he thought, maybe pride? They were his
family after all, but in all of his years he had
never felt anything like this about them and
definitely not about himself. Tears came back to
his eyes and he quickly had difficulty seeing
through them, so he sat down in the closest chair
and wiped the tear away before anyone could see
them. He had lost years of his life by running
away and it was already becoming hard to imagine
what had been so terrible that it drove him away.
It didn't matter now though because he was there
and he had work to do. Returning to the gels, he
continued draining stain until all of the gels were
solidly colored rectangular slabs in the bottoms of
otherwise empty staining trays. He then began to
pour the clear destain solution on each slab and
all of the gels were again soaking pretty quickly.
The four returned to Edward's quarters to wait out
the first wash. The washes would be short so there
would only be enough time to maybe grab something
to eat and drink before they had to return to the
lab.

A couple of washes later, the data appeared as
small dashes in the otherwise nearly transparent
sheets of gel. Walking around the lab taking a
quick look at all of the data, the four scientists
began to get a heavy feeling in the pits of their
stomachs. They had remained unsure of exactly what
they had actually expected in the data, but it
definitely wasn't what they found. Doubts flooded
in immediately and they continued to compare gel
after gel. Maybe they had made a massive mistake
loading the gels. But even that wouldn't account
for the results they were seeing. George, Ella,
and Edward had each run samples from the entire set
of bone fragments, ultimately to arrive at three
independent data sets of exactly the same
experiment, a DNA run of each of the seventy-nine
squares. The problem was, the data on the gels
looked exactly the same, and not just the
triplicates independently run from the same
original samples. They were all the same, every
single gel. Overlaying the results, they were

indisputable and could indicate only one thing.
The bone fragments were all from the same person!
The statistical probability of this particular set
of markers appearing together further indicated
that only one person who had ever lived on the
planet could have this pattern of genetic data.

The woman continued to ignore her nausea as
she searched the brick wall finding it solid from
top to bottom. When she was about to lose control
of her violently threatening stomach, a loud click
filled the air followed by the unmistakable sound
of stone grinding on stone. The woman had tripped
a switch somewhere on the wall and the entire wall
was now swinging open. The foul odor that poured
out through the gradually widening crack took her
breath away before she could stop inhaling and
pushed her nausea beyond what she could tolerate.
The whole room full of soldiers stared at the
opening that had been a brick wall a moment
earlier. None of them made a move to stop the
woman as she stumbled into the adjoining chamber
gasping for breath and vomiting bile as she went.
The gradually revealed cave beyond held the
soldiers' attentions like deer frozen in the
headlights of an approaching car. They had never
seen anything like it and probably never would
again in their lifetimes.

Eventually accepting the unexpectedly repeated
results, the four scientists now stood in front of
the wall monitor in Parker's lab waiting for their
link to be picked up by the General in the Shawnee
Nation. Captain Daniels now stood amongst the
others, the glacial ice barrier having melted into
oblivion over the course of his time in Parker's
lab. Not knowing what to think of the results
themselves, they couldn't imagine how the General
would deal with their results.
The image of an Apache soldier abruptly
snapped onto the lab's monitor, the com tech who
picked up the link speaking to someone off screen.
The General then came into their field of view, her
face grim as she spoke briskly into a headset.
"General?" Parker inquired, a little reluctant

to disturb her in her obviously tense situation. They could now hear her side of the communications over her headset and she was far from happy already.

"What?" they heard her say. She was still too distracted by what was coming through her headset and her eyes hadn't focused on them yet. Blinking rapidly several times, she appeared to realize they were on the monitor in front of her and said, "I'm sorry, Council member Parker, I just lost one of my people."

"In a farm field?" Parker asked, recalling the details of her investigation, and having difficulty believing such a thing could happen in the heart of the Nations and in a farm field of all places.

"It was an accident, a fall." She said quickly, "We're not in the field anymore." She then paused and the scientists simply stared, waiting for her to tell them more. She didn't, and a little later, Parker repeated "General?"

After another few rapid and hushed words into her headset, General Cochise seemed to fully acknowledge them, her face remaining grim. "You have results?" she asked without a change in her expression. "That was quick."

"Yes, General." Parker said, noting her mood and letting the smile fade from his face. "They aren't what we expected."

"What do you mean?" she asked, the grim look becoming a little puzzled.

"The experiments went well and we're sure of the results having done the experiment in triplicate." He said.

She now realized the captain stood right among the other three, and the overwhelming tension was only at her end of the link. "And.." she said, briefly ignoring the return of frantic chatter from her headset.

"The samples are from the same source, the same person." Parker stated, "and they could have only ever come from that one person statistically."

In the house next door to the funeral home, tension was building as the owner carried his wife into their kitchen to answer the phone.

"Is this Marcus Lemonte?" The person on the other end of the line asked as the man picked up the phone.

"Yes, this is Dr. Lemonte." He replied weakly. He had only answered the phone with a plan to hang up immediately and kill the nonstop ringing.

"This is the Shawnee Nation Investigative Unit. We understand that you own the funeral home on Restview Way. Is this true?"

In slight confusion, he recalled the flashing lights he had seen earlier and the hesitation that followed in the conversation made the agent on the other end of the line uneasy.

"Yes." Marcus said, waiting to hear the worst.

"Uhhh..doctor...if you haven't noticed out your windows, we're preparing a large scale search over here. We'd like for you to come over if you could. We will pick you up if necessary."

Pausing again, Marcus finally said, "No, no..that's O.K. I'll come over there. What's this all about? I thought you had to have a search warrant before you could search a place? I mean, I don't really care, but what the hell's going on?"

"We had a tip that the two missing boys were holed up in the funeral home. Too urgent for protocol, you can understand the circumstances, I'm sure."

Marcus paused again, but this time he heard the line go dead. It was more than he could handle tonight. For a second, he stood in the kitchen, forgetting that he had hi wife Nikki in his arms. Then the strong smell of hotdogs and popcorn returned in full force along with the feeling he was being watched. Marcus looked out the window and then into the living room. Matt must have been listening to his phone call because someone had definitely been staring at him. It wasn't just paranoia this time, it was intense and well defined. The room started to close in on him and he leaned against and slid down the wall, somehow keeping Nikki in his weakening arms. He just couldn't fit things together right now. A loud cough from the living room briefly caught his fading attention. Matt was in there, but he couldn't make it back. His attention lapsed completely, the dreaded smell became overwhelming, and he blacked out.

At the same instant in the living room, Matt's mouth twitched in anxiety. His tension and fear were again building, and he could now also feel an ungodly presence forcing its way into his perception. In desperation, he wished that it would end. But it continued, overwhelming him with terror. And then the figure from his dreams appeared! The dark figure from the corner! It now stood in the doorway to the living room, and began to gradually approach him, its shadowed face slowly becoming visible. A twisted, distorted mask appeared, and Matt realized the hideous smile was coming from Marcus's face. It hung before Matt shrouded in blackness. Tears came to his eyes as utter hopelessness swallowed him. Frozen in place, he could do nothing but stare. Suddenly, a massive rush of force swept over him, instantly crushing and shredding him to pieces before he could utter a cry or think of moving.

Floating over the bloody, nearly decapitated form that had recently been Matt, the figure shifted to face the two propped against the wall down the short hallway. Marcus remained unconscious, now in an outwardly peaceful state that hid the status epilepticus storming his brain for the first time since hospitalized following his accident. Marcus's seizure continued to drive the figure into a frenzied rage as they had ever since it had been pulled from the spirit world. Sweeping down the hall, it collected Nikki into its darkness, and abruptly vanished, appearing simultaneously in the funeral home basement holding Nikki suspended below its hideously smiling face. The sudden appearance of the figure in the already crowded basement sent the soldiers there into chaotic agitation. A scream let out in terror was instantly muffled when a massive force crushed the soldier's chest. Then there were more screams, becoming a deafening roar echoing into the small cave from behind Janet. The roar magnified the feeling of impending doom that swallowed her as soon as she entered. She clearly saw petroglyphs

covering the walls of the cave before she was
pushed deeper in as it quickly filled with
desperately screaming soldiers and the smell of
rotting bodies that swept in with them.

There expectations of compliance extremely low
even from a doctor in the Shawnee Nation, two SNIU
agents had immediately driven the short distance to
the Lemonte house to collect Marcus. Getting no
response at the front door, one had walked around
to peer through the back door into the kitchen. He
gaped in shock as a dark mass swarmed over a man
and woman propped against a wall on the kitchen
floor. The darkness abruptly disappeared with the
woman, leaving only the man slumped over and
possibly dead. Violently throwing the door open,
the agent made it to Marcus in time to feel his
thready pulse fade completely.

Her headset turning into a skull-rattling
monster, the General ripped it from her head. She
could still hear the screams over the buzz of her
ringing ears. What the hell was happening in
there! But she knew. It had gone bad like her gut
had warned her. Parker and the others in his lab
could only stare in horror at their monitor as the
scene on the other end of the link exploded into
chaos. The screaming from the headsets was
transmitted through the link, and the screaming
didn't stop. Barreling out of the command center
weapons in tow, the General and her remaining
soldiers hit the ground running and were across the
dead house lawn before they had a chance to
consider where they were going. SNIU agents and
local police who had been content with the soldiers
taking all the risk followed slowly behind the last
soldier, weapons drawn and the sweat of fear
covering their faces. The screams could be heard
from the road, and running toward them seemed wrong
to anyone still able to think. The General didn't
need to think. Her soldiers were in trouble and
she had brought them here. Once inside, they
followed the screams echoing down the massive
staircase, and made it to the top only a little
winded. The General scrambled first down the

ladder in the closet, jumping the last few feet to avoid the pile of bodies that had already been described over her headset. Counting three soldiers down already, she felt immediate guilt for being too late to save them. Unfortunately, the timing of her arrival was otherwise impeccable.

The instant Marcus Lemonte died, the dark figure was ripped through the back wall of the petroglyph covered cave, returning explosively to the spirit world it had escaped when Marcus had died following the accident and had been revived. Not having the total life support of an ICU this time, Marcus would not be returning. As the figure disappeared into the wall, a careening soldier caught the woman the figure had been holding in mid air. The clap of thunder caused by its return to the land of the dead blasted everyone in the cave and the attached room off their feet. They all remained on the ground for a while overwhelmed by the shock of the past few moments. Slowly, the realization that it was over came to them all, their minds already struggling to barricade the event out of remembrance to preserve their sanity. Even the open-minded soldiers with extensive spiritual beliefs would have trouble with this one. It was the making of nightmares and the future thief of sleep.

The General scanned the floor for anyone not moving and counted two soldiers with heads mangled almost beyond recognition. She realized she had lost Captain Atwell and one other besides the first at the ladder, but the rest were alive. Maybe not well, but alive.

One of the last to stand up, the woman who had led her soldiers in caught sight of the two mangled soldiers that had fallen to the figure. The General stood over them and the woman saw that her demeanor was no longer that of the person in command she had pleaded to not long before. Regardless of everything else the General may have been, she continued to be human and she felt loss.

The woman then staggered over to the only other civilian among the crowd. The soldier who had caught Nikki was then able to buffer her in the fall when they were knocked down by the concussive blast. She was now standing, but she appeared to be stunned or in some form of shock. Janet recognized the other woman from the single visit she had made with her husband to the realty office concerning the funeral home. There was a dramatic decline in her appearance, but the woman was Mrs. Lemonte. She felt pretty sure of it for some reason.

Gently grasping her arm, the woman tried to connect with Mrs. Lemonte. "Mrs. Lemonte…are you alright?" But Mrs. Lemonte only stared at her without seeing. There was no point in pursuing her concern or trying to explain why she was here among this mess in the Lemontes' funeral home. Mrs. Lemonte wouldn't understand and probably wouldn't believe her if she did. If she had been alone to witness this and then tried to describe it to her own son, he would have had her locked away like her old uncle. The thought was vaguely comforting. Maybe her uncle hadn't been crazy after all.

Walking next to stand by the General, the woman observed the ragged mess the figure had made of the two soldiers. The General didn't move or acknowledge in any way that she was there, but it felt like the right thing to do and the woman stood there until the soldiers forced her to leave the Pit. Remarkably, someone had already given it that name, and it seemed more appropriate than anything else.

Back up the ladder, the woman was briefly blinded by an array of spotlights the SNIU had already carried up into the hallway. At least they could handle a little manual labor. None of them had gone into the Pit, and when none of them would even meet her gaze, she realized they had no intention of ever going down there. If she was being generous, she could chalk it up to wisdom on their part, but they didn't seem to deserve her generosity.

Again remembering the man she had left there after the party, the woman made her way down the well-lit hall. She came across a couple of pools of dried blood, but the guy definitely wasn't in the hall. Quick checks of the half dozen rooms on

the second floor revealed nothing, no more blood
and no bodies. She felt a little relieved until
she imagined him being part of the mass of rotting
bodies in the Pit. That thought drove her out of
the funeral home and over to her car. She didn't
leave, she just felt better in something large,
solid and familiar.

CHAPTER 14

The following several weeks were spent trying
to explain the unexplainable both to themselves and
to anyone else who would listen. The media was
again unavoidable, the whole train of vans having
followed the Apache mobile command center
immediately to Hawthorne from the farm field.
Welcome or not, they had to be dealt with, but
General Cochise wouldn't speak to anyone, not even
the NNS as usual. The loss of three more of her
soldiers in peacetime hit her hard, particularly
the loss of Atwell. She had come to like and
respect Atwell for some strange reason having spent
the last few days of his life with him. She found
herself reacting to his death more intensely than
she even had to Ilya O'Connor's, and that death had
shaken the entire Intertribal Council. She had
felt O'Connor's death was personal until then. She
had known Atwell and that was personal.

The General remained in Hawthorne through the
following weeks with a few of her soldiers, the
fully expanded command center still sitting on the
road in front of the dead house. She hadn't gone
back into the dead house for dozens of reasons, but
teams from all over the Nations were scouring the
cave uncovered over the course of the nightmare.
At some time in the past, the cave had clearly been
accessible from the surface. The builders of the
dead house had apparently come across the buried
cave during construction of a basement for the
funeral home, and the new owner of the land, a
Pierre Lemonte, had hoarded the find with a zeal
generally found in gold prospectors. There was no
telling what ancient native artifacts he had

unearthed and sold to build his wealth. No doubt greedy European immigrants whose cultural treasures remained safe across the ocean had similarly desecrated Cahokia. But both the newly found cave and Cahokia would be preserved from then on in memory of the ancients.

Per expert opinion, the petroglyphs in the cave predated the Mississippian culture, and were probably done by the first inhabitants of the continent prior to the Adena and Hopewell cultures, making them the oldest Native relics found to date. Initial interpretation of the cave writings suggested the cave wall was a connection or bridge to the spirit world. Further translation of the cave was already well under way, and had amazingly been given a major leap by the scrawlings of an old man who had worked for the Lemontes in his earlier years. How he had managed to interpret them was unknown, but he had reportedly died in a nursing home in the recent past and sent the parchment to his only known relative in the Nations. Not by coincidence, the relative, Janet Portraire, was the same person who had led the General's soldiers through the dead house when the cave was rediscovered. Janet had been tasked by her old uncle with closing the gate and stopping the spirits, neither of them knowing that the gate could never be closed. The spirit world was integrally related to her own, overlapping and apparently intersecting it at numerous places in the universe, notably places known for their mystical or religious power. At least that was the theory being touted by anyone with an interest in the subject. The suspected sites were too numerous to list, but among the ones postulated were Stonehenge and Easter Island. Modern evidence of their significance hadn't been definitively documented until then. Skeptics still abounded of course, but having seen the dark spirit pass into the cave wall with a clap of thunder that knocked her off her feet, the General's belief in the spirit world had been greatly enhanced. She didn't exactly have a choice in the matter.

The General spent a large part of her time in Hawthorne speaking to the woman, Janet, who had gone into the dead house with her soldiers. Janet was exceptional when it came to diverting the media away from her and that was nearly priceless. She also had the guts of an Apache soldier with an additional benefit of not fearing the dead. The General liked her almost immediately and that was rare. It could have been because they experienced the same bizarre and horrific event, but the connection had most likely been there before that when Janet asked for the opportunity to go into the dead house, something the General couldn't imagine ever doing herself.

The General's presence during the traumatic event brought a tremendous amount of credibility to the story Janet repeatedly had to tell the media and other investigators. Without her support, Janet believed she would have been locked away like her old uncle.

The rediscovery of the Pit brought team after team of investigators to Hawthorne, and they all wanted first hand accounts from Janet, the only coherent civilian who witnessed the event in the cave, and the only person who was talking. It got old quickly, but there was talk of a book deal and she needed the money now that Norman was out of the picture. Work was a little scarce in Hawthorne. But she had grown up here and she couldn't imagine leaving.

In terms of the dark spirit, little could be said for certain. Two soldiers from her forensic teams who were of northern Algonquian decent believed the spirit was the nightmarish Windigo of their myths. It had similarities to the dark spirit with both of them shredding their victims apart in shrieking fits of rage. But all of those who witnessed it claimed the figure had a face that monstrously resembled the doctor who had lived next door, actually owned the dead house, and apparently died around the same time the figure left the world through the cave wall. According to the SNIU agent who found the dying doctor, the dark figure somehow transported the doctor's wife out of their house next door. That same figure then appeared in the cave with the woman out of nowhere. The General trusted her soldiers' reports and her own eyes in that regard, traumatized or not. The most notable thing about the dark spirit was that it was a killer, and possibly the one she had been hunting. The evidence of that was still fresh in her soldiers' minds, and bore a clear and disturbing resemblance to the deaths she had already been investigating. The obvious increase in ferocity remained a significant difference from the bodies they had found, but the rest of the puzzle seemed to fall into place with a little effort and imagination.

The General's investigation connected further with those horrible events by way of the bone fragments found at the excavated dumpsites of the bodies they had recovered. All of the bone fragments were unexpectedly from the same source. They would have never made a connection if the doctor hadn't died next door and underwent not only an autopsy, but also a subsequent genetic analysis by Parker's lab because of the reportedly bizarre facial similarity the doctor had to the dark spirit. According to Parker, Marcus Lemonte's marker pattern overlaid those from the bone squares without a single difference. Considering the statistical probability of that no matter how unreasonable it sounded, science seemed to eliminate any guesswork. But where had all of that bone come from while he was still a living, breathing and highly functional individual? It was still a mystery. With the information Janet had been able to gather from the doctor's widow, the only possible source for the bone was a skull section removed following a traumatic accident he had somehow survived on the Internation highway. His autopsy revealed a metal plate that replaced a significant area of his skull damaged in the accident. How and why that skull fragment was turned into or actually crafted into all of those little square pieces per captain Daniels and then meticulously placed for them to recover at their excavations, they would probably never know.

Beyond that, the General would do her best to be hopeful that the series of murders had been ended in the Nations. Of course, as she repeatedly mentioned in the past, she was not an optimist.

179

Therefore, she would wait for the worst.

THE END

ABOUT THE AUTHOR

The author currently lives with his wife and daughter in Las Vegas. He hasn't decided if there will be a Las Vegas in the Ravaging Myths world yet, but is open to suggestions.

www.ingramcontent.com/pod-product-compliance
Lightning Source LLC
Chambersburg PA
CBHW050941120626
46552CB00001B/321